THE M

RICH BOTTLES JR.

THE MANACLED

a.k.a. – ZILF

RICH BOTTLES JR.

Burning Bulb
PUBLISHING

The Manacled
By **Rich Bottles Jr.**

Published in association with:

Burning Bulb Publishing
P.O. Box 4721
Bridgeport, WV 26330-4721
www.BurningBulbPublishing.com

Edition ISBN

   Paperback 978-0-61567-356-1

First edition.
Printed in the United States of America.

Library of Congress Control Number: 2012944927

Dedicated to:

Anyone who purchased

"Lumberjacked" or *"Hellhole West Virginia."*

Stoop not down, therefore
Unto the Darkly Splendid
World.
Wherein continually liveth
A fruitless depth
And Hades wrapped
In cloud
Delighting in images
A black, ever-rolling
Abyss
Formless
And Void.

> \- H.P. Lovecraft, as quoted by a West Virginia State Penitentiary inmate on his cell wall: Floor 1 Block A Cell 3

I've chased my dreams
And seen them die.
I've had lovers
But had to say good bye...
I've trusted some
And got burned.
I could write a book
With all I've learned.
We once were close
But time pushed us apart.
Now we're left healing,
Healing a broken heart!!!

- Written on the wall: Floor 1 Block A
  Cell 11

"Bless me Father, for I have sinned. It has been at least two years since my last confession."

"Blessed is our God, at all times, now and always and forever and ever. Amen... But why have you waited two years to come back for confession?"

"I have been trying desperately to save my daughter from a life of sin, but have now realized that I cannot do it alone. I confess to the mortal sin of failing to raise my daughter according to the Catholic teachings."

"Failing indicates that you have *tried* to correct her, so I can assure you that you have not committed a mortal sin. But tell me more of your problems with the child."

"Ever since my husband passed, she has become wilder and more out of control. She refuses to go to school or church, she blasphemes the Lord and curses me, she marks her body with unholy tattoos and sometimes doesn't come home for days at a time. She is seventeen now and I fear that she will move out of the house next year and I'll lose her forever."

"It sounds as though it is your daughter who should be seeking penance and not you. You cannot use this sacrament to obtain reconciliation of another's sins."

daughter

"I know that, Father. Perhaps the Confessional grill is the wrong place to seek the Church's help…"

"I can pray with you for your daughter's healing, but unless she is willing to meet with me or perhaps one of our youth ministers, I don't know what other counsel we can provide. We do offer support groups and family counseling, but the child needs to *participate* for it to be effective."

"I'm afraid she needs more than prayers and counseling, Father… and I know this sounds crazy, but I think she needs an exorcism."

"Exorcism is an ancient ritual, regardless of how Hollywood may portray it. Besides, the Catholic Church would not entertain the thought of performing an exorcism just because a child gets a tattoo, stays out late or dishonors her mother."

"Please don't trivialize my predicament, Father. The tattoos are pentagrams and inverted crosses. Plus, I have heard my daughter speak in a foreign tongue."

"The language?"

"Yes, very foul language."

"I mean, what foreign language does she speak?"

"I have no idea what it is. It almost sounds Indian, like those alternative lyrics at the bottom of '*Amazing Grace*' in the hymnals."

"But you're not sure, right? It could just be some made up babbling, or something she may have picked up on the streets."

"No, I don't know exactly what language it is. I'm not the one who is possessed. But it's certainly not babbling, slang, Ebonics or *whatever else you're inferring*."

3

"Please calm down. I'm only trying to better understand the situation so that we can find the best solution. But I strongly believe we need to steer clear of the suggestion of diabolic possession."

"My family has been attending Saint Joseph's for generations. I was baptized here and my daughter was baptized here. My husband received his Last Rites from Father Ronnecamps and his funeral was held here in the Cathedral. So why can't you help me now with this Catholic Rite?"

"I just need you to realize that even the suggestion of an exorcism to one who is mentally afflicted can do more harm than good. If a person does not have faith in the theology behind the Rite, the fine line between mental and spiritual well-being becomes blurred... Thus, we need to seek out and investigate other options in order to help your daughter... You have to trust me on this... Will you at least join me in prayer?... We can pray in the name of Jesus Christ that your daughter be protected against the power of evil forces... Are you still there?... Go in peace."

Standing beneath a street light next to a Chapline Street row house was a tall young man dressed in a black cloak with a matching wide-rimmed Parson's hat. Clutched in his right hand was a black leather field specialist medical bag. The evening fog rolling off the nearby Ohio River seemed to gather around his japanned footwear and definitely would have added to the ominous scene had the Wheeling Public Works Department replaced the faulty street lamp.

"I have to use the camera light because it's too dark," explained the man's stocky partner, who sported a black leather jacket and ill-fitting slacks.

"Never mind then," the man impatiently answered. "Just try to get an exterior shot of the house before we go in."

"We could try to move up the street a bit for your fog shot."

"Never mind I said. Would you just capture the exterior like I asked?"

After a few minutes of fumbling with the Canon 1172 video camera, the shorter man motioned that he was finished and the pair proceeded up a few cement stairs toward the porch of a brightly-painted blue sandstone Victorian home.

"At least there's not many stairs if you was to fall, because of the fog, I mean," the cameraman mumbled as he walked behind the black-cloaked man.

A quick tap on the front door was promptly met with a curious response of "May I help you?" as a middle-aged-looking woman in a floral housedress espied her evening visitors with apprehension. The woman was actually in her late thirties, but years of worry and turmoil in raising her teenage daughter had taken their toll.

"Mrs. Schmulbach? We're priests from St. Joseph's. May we come in?"

"I suppose."

The woman stepped aside to allow the men to cross the threshold. The lead priest maintained a serious countenance as he passed, removing his hat in the process, while the second man displayed an awkward smile. Both men's faces had dark complexions and indicated a Mideastern descent.

"Please have a seat in the living room," she invited as she closed the door. "I so dislike Daylight Saving Time. The days get shorter and the temperatures get colder. I'm used to it still being daylight at this time."

The living room was conservatively decorated and the sparse furnishings made the room look larger than it was. Both men sat on a faux leather sofa and waited until the woman sat in an adjacent recliner. The shorter man placed his camera securely on his lap, maintaining his uneasy smile.

"Are you boys from around here?"

"Actually, we're both from McMechen. My name is Father Joseph and this is Brother Theodore."

"Oh my," responded the woman. "My mother told me nothing good can ever come out of McMechen, but I guess you two proved her wrong. You even share a name with the Cathedral."

"Well, both my parents wanted to call me James, but they disagreed on which apostle James I should be named after, so they eventually settled on Joseph."

Brother Theodore chuckled nervously when he saw the perplexed look on the woman's face.

After an uncomfortable silence, Joseph continued, "Be that as it may, last week Father Frobass asked us to drop by and discuss the problems you're having with your daughter. I pray we're not intruding or over-stepping our bounds by showing up here unannounced."

"Oh, not at all, but I thought the Church wanted nothing to do with me once I broached the subject of exorcism. I hope you're not here just to reiterate the displeasure I encountered last week at the Confessional."

"No, no, no," Father Joseph quickly answered, choosing to place his leather bag on the coffee table in front of him at that precise moment, "in fact, just the opposite. You see, the last *official Church-sanctioned* exorcism in the United States was over fifty years ago, but that didn't stop the Vatican from revising the Rite of Exorcism canon twice during the nineteen-nineties and then requiring every Diocese to staff a trained exorcist. So yes, the Liturgy of Exorcism is obviously alive and well within the Catholic Church, but there are strict rules stating that exorcisms must never be reported in any media and should be treated with extreme discretion."

"So that's why Father Frobass was reluctant to discuss the matter with me directly?"

"Exactly," Joseph confirmed. "Exorcism is a sacrament, established by Jesus Christ, where the Church protects His children from the Evil One. It was Father Frobass who recommended that we come see you."

"Well, in that case, why don't you gentlemen take your coats off and stay awhile? Perhaps, I can get you some coffee or tea?"

The woman rose when she saw the men stand up to remove their coats, but sat back down when Joseph indicated that refreshments were not necessary. "May we place our garments on this chair?"

"Certainly."

Once everyone was sitting again, Joseph announced, "We shall look for signs of the Diabolic when we meet your daughter, but first we'd like to ask you some questions to determine how she may have become afflicted."

When Mrs. Schmulbach noticed the shorter man making adjustments to his video camera, she asked, "You're going to film this?"

"Yes, ma'am," calmly answered Joseph, "but please do not be alarmed. Remember what I said about being discreet. Theodore is my assistant and it is his job to create a record of our meetings. It is required by the Church and is meant to protect the Church against false claims – and it may serve as a learning tool for priests studying the Rite of Exorcism. But if the video is ever shown outside the Wheeling-Charleston Diocese, I assure you that your family name will not be associated with it and your faces will not be discernible."

"I guess that's all right," she answered while straightening the collar on her housedress and making sure all the buttons down the front were secure.

"We're filming," whispered Theodore.

The trio's attention was directed upward at a lighted ceiling fan, which suddenly started rhythmically screeching as if it had suddenly been kicked off balance like a clothes washer containing too many soccer shoes. A dull methodic thumping could also be heard coming from the room above.

"First meeting at the home of the afflicted in Wheeling, West Virginia, November seventh, approximately nineteen-hundred hours: My name is Father Joseph and I am here with the mother of the afflicted and my assistant Brother Theodore...Ma'am, has your daughter recently been involved in any type of violence, illicit drug use or sexual perversion?"

"I don't believe so… sexual perversion, though? Are you serious?"

"This *is* West Virginia, ma'am."

"If she's taking drugs or having sexual relations, then she's hiding it from me."

"Would you know if she recently had an abortion?"

"Oh my god, I hope not!"

"So do we, ma'am, so do we. The spiritual repercussions of abortion can exasperate and embolden the Diabolic… But to continue on, do you have any reason to believe that your daughter could be the victim of a curse or a spell?"

"No, that's ridiculous… at least, I think that's ridiculous. Do you gentlemen come across that a lot around here?"

"Unfortunately, the Internet, along with the television programs, motion pictures and music of today, has influenced many youth to experiment with the occult and black magic. As Christians, we believe that nothing happens without the knowledge of the Divine and that evil is allowed to exist. But as humans, we are also given the freedom to choose. Some choose to follow Christ, while others choose to worship at the altar of a demonic mass media."

The silence from Mrs. Schmulbach accentuated the noise from the wobbling fan blades and the dull beats emanating from the ceiling. After awhile, a blush came over the face of Mrs. Schmulbach and she began sobbing. "I'm afraid my daughter listens to the type of evil music you describe, but I didn't really see any harm in it. I couldn't even understand the words. I'm so ashamed."

"Now, now, let's try to keep our composure for your daughter's sake. No one is here to judge you or your daughter. We consider you both as victims and we are here to help."

"Thank you, Father, I will do whatever you need me to do in order to save my daughter."

"Well, maybe we'll take you up on that offer of hot tea before we go upstairs to meet your daughter."

While the woman busied herself out of sight in the kitchen, preparing tea for her guests, Father Joseph jammed his index finger inside his white clerical collar and encircled his sweaty neck to loosen it up. "She must have the furnace on full blast in here and that ceiling fan isn't doing much to circulate the air."

Joseph searched through his valise, verifying that everything was there that he would need. He placed the bag back onto the floor, making room for the refreshments that Mrs. Schmulbach was preparing.

"You shoulda asked for iced tea," Theodore suggested.

Soon the clinking of metal spoons stirring inside china cups accompanied the duller noise from above, as the fan continued to make its laborious rounds and the muted music continued to pound through the ceiling.

"Very nice home you have here, Mrs. Schmulbach," Joseph announced between sips.

"Why thank you, Father, it's a Victorian style house, built in the late eighteen-hundreds. It's on the National Register of Historic Places."

"You've kept it up well."

"I assume your accommodations are suitable?"

"We live humbly, in a quiet place," Father Joseph answered, glancing momentarily at the ceiling. "Not a lot of... distractions."

Mrs. Schmulbach looked over to Brother Theodore and smiled. "You don't say a whole lot do you, Brother Theodore?"

"He's a bit of an introvert," volunteered Father Joseph, "although he will get into a rant if he's passionate enough about something."

Brother Theodore took a sip from the cup shaking in his hand, and then stabilized it with his other hand as he brought it away from his mouth. "Nice house you got here," he said.

After a brief pause, Mrs. Schmulbach responded, "How very nice of you to notice."

"Is it perhaps Victorian?" asked Theodore.

Father Joseph suddenly clapped his hands together and said, "All right then, how about we go upstairs to meet your daughter?"

The carpet-covered stairs allowed the trio to creep up the steps silently, although the thudding music coming from above would've allowed Pope John XXIII to make a surreptitious approach. Mrs. Schmulbach led the way, while Brother Theodore brought up the rear, clumsily filming the rears of those preceding him.

Halfway down the hall on the second floor, the woman stopped in front of a red door with a plastic sign thumb-tacked to the center, warning, "DO NOT DISTURB – Stören Sie Nicht!"

The bottom of the sign bounced and reverberated against the door with each drum beat, while the chanting lyrics of '*Infect the Masses*' bled out from the threshold.

"What is your daughter's name?" whispered Father Joseph.

In-fect the mah-sez!

"Excuse me?"

In-fect the mah-sez!

"What is your daughter's name?"

In-fect the mah-sez!

"Why are we whispering?" asked Brother Theodore.

In-fect the mah-sez!

Raising his voice a bit, Father Joseph repeated, "What... is... your... daugh-ter's... name?"

In-fect the mah-sez!

"Oh, Kennedy; my daughter's name is Kennedy Schmulbach."

In-fect the mah-sez!

"Okay, perhaps just you and I should go in," *-fect the mah-sez!* "at first, anyway, Mrs. Schmulbach, so that the camera doesn't upset Kennedy."

In-fect the mah-sez!

"Yes, that would be a very good idea. In fact," *the mah-sez!* "I was just going to suggest that."

In-fect the mah-sez!

"Also, please do not mention anything directly or indirect," *the mah!* "-say, about exorcisms. We should just refer to this visit as..." *In-fect the mah-sez!* "sort-of a spiritual intervention."

In-fect the mah-sez!

Without bothering to knock, which would've been senseless, Mrs. Schmulbach twisted the door knob and entered the room, followed by Father Joseph. Brother Theodore was careful to stay out of the doorway, so that he couldn't be seen from inside the room. The door was left open however, so that the teen wouldn't feel entrapped.

The bedroom was dark, lit only by some candles scattered around the room. Kennedy was lying on her back on the bed, her head propped up on some pillows. When she peripherally saw the light of the hallway splash into the room, she quickly twisted her head around (but not more so than a normal human would, of course), in order to see the intruders. Through long brown strands of hair, which draped haphazardly in front of her half-covered face, she glared intently as her mother and the priest approached the bed.

"Could you turn the music off, hon'?" Mrs. Schmulbach asked with a raised voice. "We'd like to talk to you."

Kennedy slowly raised a pajama-cloaked arm off the bed and aimed a small remote at a stereo console across the room. With a sudden twist of the wrist, she turned the music off and allowed the remote to bounce onto the bed beside her. But she kept her eyes on the visitors the whole time, until they separated and took stations on opposite sides of the bed.

She watched suspiciously as the priest placed a black bag on the bed near her bare feet. She wondered if the priest was secretly checking out her skinny legs, since all she wore were some black silk shorts and a red button-up pajama top.

"Hello, Kennedy, I'm Father Joseph. I was visiting your mom this evening and I thought I'd come up to say hello to you."

Kennedy looked up at her mother and hissed, "Is this some kind of stupid intervention?"

Mrs. Schmulbach nervously laughed and moved some of the disheveled hair away from her daughter's face. "Of course not, honey, the Father just wants to visit with you."

"Visit my ass!" Kennedy blurted.

Father Joseph smiled down at the youth as mom exclaimed, "Kennedy!"

"Hey," Father Joseph said, still smiling, "that was some kind of wild music you were listening to. What was that anyway?"

"S.T.D.," she sneered.

"Excuse me?"

"The band is called S.T.D.," she repeated, pointing to a poster on the wall of an angry, bare-chested, boney, red-haired singer with his fist lifted triumphantly toward the sky. The singer's free hand was wrapped tightly around the top of a microphone stand. Across the top of the poster was a red-lettered banner stating "DAMIEN SATAN."

"And the song I heard was called '*Infect the Masses*'?" he guessed. "I wish I could excite my masses like that young man obviously can."

"Maybe you could if you worshipped Satan like he does. Damien excites my masses!" she proudly announced while wiggling her torso on the bed, causing her burgeoning breasts to grind feverishly against the inside of her top and creating the threat of some buttons bursting off.

"Calm yourself down, dear," cautioned Mrs. Schmulbach, "Father Joseph doesn't want to see your boobies."

"Bullshit!"

"Well, be that as it may," circumvented Father Joseph. "Don't you think some types of music can be harmful to the soul or a person's well-being?"

"You mean like Country music?"

"Not necessarily, but I believe music is like most things we find pleasurable – when enjoyed in moderation, many things are not harmful, but it is possible to have too much of a good thing."

"Like religion?"

"You're obviously a very sharp and intelligent young lady. The point I'm trying to make is that it's a lot easier to get introduced into an unhealthy culture, say through music or drug experimentation, than it is to escape from such a culture."

"I don't take drugs."

"I didn't say that you did. I was just making a…"

"I drink a lot though. I love to get drunk."

"Kennedy! Don't tell the priest lies," chastised Mrs. Schmulbach.

"I'm not lying; I'll drink anything that has alcohol in it. And plenty of it."

"So you admit you have a problem?" asked Father Joseph.

"I have a problem with you bein' here preachin' at me. That's the only problem I have. I knew this was some kind of fuckin' intervention!"

"Kennedy!"

"Maybe we should change the subject, since I don't want our visit to turn adversarial."

"No, we wouldn't want that," agreed Kennedy.

"Let's get back to your intellect, Kennedy," Father Joseph suggested. "I bet you know some things that neither your mother nor I know about. Do you have knowledge of anything obscure or unusual?"

"Well, that's why we have the Internet; perhaps you could explain that concept to my mom."

"No, no, that's not the kind of information I'm talking about. I mean personal things or secret things."

"So what's this have to do with intellect? Sounds like you're trying to trick me into revealing something by complimenting me."

"I'm sorry if you interpreted my praise the wrong way. I honestly do believe you're a smart girl."

After a few moments of stubborn silence, Kennedy looked up at the priest and admitted, "Well, I do know where your car keys are."

"My car keys?"

"Yeah, the ones you thought you lost awhile ago."

"Now you're beginning to intrigue me. Tell me what happened to my keys."

Kennedy grinned, "Your keys are lost up some poor altar boy's ass!"

"Kennedy! You apologize to Father Joseph this instant!"

Father Joseph chuckled in a dismissive sort of way and said, "That won't be necessary, Mrs. Schmulbach." He leaned over the bed and lightly whispered into Kennedy's ear, trying to ensure that the girl's mother couldn't hear, "*Would I be looking at your legs if I was interested in boys?*"

Kennedy sat up suddenly and began nasally shouting, "Sasháék! Ne' aknöhsút tkanôke' ne wátsí! Tësta't! Ehsenyusyúta't! Tësta't! Ehsenyusyúta't! Tësta't! Ehsenyusyúta't! Tesaskéyô? Twayatë's!"

"Oh my god!" gasped Mrs. Schmulbach.

"Tësta't! Ehsenyusyúta't! Tësta't! Ehsenyusyúta't! Tësta't! Ehsenyusyúta't!"

Father Joseph was shaken by the outburst, but tried to remain calm as he patiently reached for his satchel. After digging around briefly inside the bag, he produced two bright violet cloth stoles. He quickly wrapped one stole around his neck and handed the other to Mrs. Schmulbach.

"Tesaskéyô? Twayatë's!"

Mrs. Schmulbach looked queerly at the scarf-like stole, especially the knotted loop at one end, but realized the urgency of the situation and swung the cloth around the back of her neck like the priest had done.

"I think we need to pray together," announced Father Joseph, grasping the girl's right hand as tightly as he could. Mrs. Schmulbach quickly swooped in to grab the girl's other hand. Kennedy tried to pull one of her hands free, but couldn't muster the strength from her reclining position.

"Watch me!" directed the priest, making eye contact with Mrs. Schmulbach.

With his free hand, the priest pulled the stole off his neck near the knotted loop and brought it down deliberately near his other hand. Maintaining pressure on the girl's wrist, he wrapped the loop around her hand and tightened the knot. He then yanked the girl's arm above her head, let go of her bound wrist and tied the free end of the stole onto the nearest bed post.

Mrs. Schmulbach's initial confusion caused her to have more trouble holding onto Kennedy's free hand as the girl began struggling violently. Father Joseph raced around the foot of the bed to provide assistance to the woman.

"What the fuck are you doing?! Let me go, you fuckers!" screamed the girl.

The priest eventually got the girl's other hand tied to the second bed post, but the teen soon started bouncing on the mattress, kicking her legs and twisting her body. She then made contact with the priest's bag and kicked it to the floor.

"We've got to secure her legs before she hurts herself or breaks the bed," warned the priest as he hustled to retrieve his bag. After leaning over and fumbling momentarily with the bag, he straightened back up holding two more looped stoles in his hand.

"Hold her leg while I get this on!" he commanded.

"Is this really necessary, Father?" Mrs. Schmulbach asked desperately, but still followed the man's directions.

"Hell no, it's not necessary!" shrieked Kennedy. "Let me go or I'm gonna call child protective services!"

When the teen was finally tied spread-eagle across the bed, Father Joseph pulled a handkerchief from his shirt pocket and wiped his sweaty brow. "I need to talk to you, privately, Mrs. Schmulbach."

As the two adults began walking away from the bed, he added, "Kennedy, you wait here."

Joining Brother Theodore in the hallway, Father Joseph pulled the bedroom door shut. He dried his forehead once more before stuffing the damp handkerchief back into his pocket.

"I think I got a lot of the talking recorded on the audio," Theodore proudly announced to deaf ears.

"What's going on Father? I didn't expect anything like this. Is my daughter going to be all right?"

"What did you expect an exorcism to be like, Mrs. Schmulbach? Speaking in foreign tongues is a clear sign of diabolic possession. Thankfully, whatever evil is possessing your daughter doesn't appear to be very strong at this point. Usually, it's much more difficult restraining the victim."

"What language was that anyway?"

"Unfortunately, I haven't a clue, Mrs. Schmulbach."

"If I may offer some circumflex observations," offered Theodore in circumspect. "Judging from the acute and grave accents I heard coming from the room, not to mention the umlauts, I might suggest a Native American origin."

"You might?" rhetorically asked Joseph.

"I also didn't hear any R sounds."

19

Father Joseph and Mrs. Schmulbach stared at Theodore, until he looked down and pretended to adjust his camera.

"As I said, I don't have a clue what language she was speaking in there, but it didn't sound made up and it seemed like something that would take some practice to duplicate. That's why I felt it was urgent to secure her to the bed so that I could begin the formal Rite of Exorcism."

"Well, I guess you know what you're doing…"

"Of course I do, Mrs. Schmulbach. Now, Brother Theodore and I are going to enter Kennedy's bedroom and begin the ritual. It is best that you stay away during this stage, so the spirit does not attempt to exploit your, uh, nurturing instinct. Regardless of what you may hear coming from this room, it is imperative for you to leave us alone. I have faith that we can save your daughter, but you must follow my directions and let us work our miracles."

"I will, Father; I trust you, Father," cried the woman. "God bless you and thank you for helping us."

Mrs. Schmulbach began fishing around in the pocket of her housedress until she produced a Rosary, which had ten thick plastic heart-shaped beads attached and a metal crucifix at the bottom of the string. "Please give this to my baby, if it will help."

When Father Joseph opened the door, he saw that the room was pitch black and he immediately realized that the candles had been extinguished. "The candles must have blown out when I shut the door," he said to Theodore over his shoulder. "Let me find the light switch."

"I could record in infrared," Theodore pointlessly volunteered as Joseph switched on the ceiling light, revealing Kennedy waiting quietly on the bed. Theodore managed to kick the door shut while focusing the camera.

"Sorry I left you in the dark," Father Joseph greeted as he approached the bed.

Kennedy now had tears in her eyes and appeared to be shaking uncontrollably. Her long hair had partially covered her face again, but she had no way to pull it back by herself.

"Please let me go," she sobbed. "I promise I'll be good. I'll help with the dishes and laundry, whatever my mom wants. I'll finish school too. Just untie me, please."

Brother Theodore felt pity for the waif as he viddied her through the viewfinder, especially since Father Joseph completely ignored her appeals. Joseph kept eye contact with the girl as he leaned down, picked up his bag and purposely placed it back onto the mattress.

"Why are you filming this? Please stop. I don't want to be filmed."

Joseph back-handed her cheek with such force that tears, snot and spit sprayed from her face across the pillow. "Shut the fuck up!" he commanded.

But she didn't shut the fuck up, screaming out, "Mom! Mom! Help me please! Mom!"

The man quickly grabbed his bag, found a roll of duct tape, and pulled the soiled handkerchief out of his pocket. The girl continued to tug and struggle against the bindings, which held her body against the bed, like a scared monkey awaiting a vivisection.

"Your mom's not going to help you," Joseph explained as he stuffed the balled-up handkerchief into her mouth and secured it with a strip of duct tape.

The girl immediately began gagging on the cloth as the saliva in her mouth mixed with the man's stale sweat. After an unsavory gulp, she resigned herself to sobbing silently under her restraints.

Joseph glanced around the room until he spied a wooden chair next to a computer desk. Without hesitation, he retrieved the chair, walked over to the door and jammed the top of the chair under the door knob. The girl watched him secure the door through tear-drenched eyes.

When Joseph returned to the bed, he grinned down at Kennedy and said, "Now where were we? Oh yes, I remember, earlier you invited me to visit your ass."

He produced a pocket knife from his pants and flicked the blade open, waving it about maliciously in the hope that the camera would pick up on some flashes and glare from the shiny metal.

Leaning over the foot of the bed, he placed the blade under the knotted stole near Kennedy's left ankle. "Perhaps I should cut you loose, because you seem sincere about being a good girl from now on. Would you like that?"

She nodded her head in the affirmative.

"But then again," added Joseph, pulling the blade away from the cloth, "you might not learn your lesson unless you're properly punished for the things you did while you were a bad girl."

Kennedy tried to say 'please,' but her muffled voice sounded like the audio of an adult cable TV channel which required a subscription to unscramble.

Joseph circled around the side of the bed, but made sure he kept the knife blade close to the girl's leg. He crouched down to place his head near her calf, so that she could feel his breath on her skin, and then accented her sensory experience by placing the tip of the knife just above her ankle. The girl's legs began trembling and she tried to raise her head to see what was happening, but the back of the man's head was in the way.

He slowly began to drag the tip of the blade up the girl's leg, applying just enough pressure to scratch her skin without causing any bleeding. "Be careful not to move your leg too much, this heathen blade can be very unforgiving."

As the knife moved near her knee, he continued to move his head accordingly, in order to watch the progress as closely as possible the wet warmth of his breath being consistently sliced by the cold touch of hardened steel. When he felt the girl's shorts touch the back of his ear, he leaned up but continued to draw the blade up her thigh.

Then she felt the blade slip under the leg opening of her silk shorts.

"Are you ready to be punished for being a bad girl?"

Kennedy shook her head back and forth and tried to plead with her eyes.

"But you have been a bad girl, haven't you?"

This time Joseph responded to her muted negative reply by clutching the fabric of her shorts into a ball with his left hand. "Well, you must be a bad girl, because good girls do not get tied to their beds and have knives poking at their pussies."

In one swift coordinated motion, a flick of his right wrist tore through the crumpled silk and allowed Joseph to pull the sliced shorts out from under the girl's ass. A barely-trimmed crotch was revealed to Joseph and the camera. The corner of a tattoo was also visible, spilling out from under the bottom of the girl's shirt.

"It looks like we have some kind of funky body art too," observed Joseph as he snapped shut his knife and re-deposited it into his pants. "Of course, good girls usually don't desecrate their bodies with tattoos either. Let's take a closer look, shall we?"

Joseph began unbuttoning the girl's shirt from the bottom, exposing an inverted crucifix tattoo, which began just under her navel and ended beyond the hair line of her pubic region, thus making it appear that the savior on the upside down cross had a furry afro sprouting from his thorny crown.

"That's just nasty, Kennedy," Joseph commented as he continued unbuttoning the shirt. "And what do we have here?"

As Joseph spread open the shirt on both sides of her pale chest, two more tattoos were visible in the main focal area. On the crest of each creamery breast was a bright green tattoo encircling a pink protruding nipple, forming the unmistakable shape of a pentagram.

"Really, Kennedy, pentacles on your titties? I hope you didn't plan to ever nurse a baby with those sacrilegious sacs."

He roughly cupped her left breast with his right hand and dipped down to suck hard on her exposed nipple. When the fingers of his left hand found their way to her other nipple and began twisting and tugging the bud, Kennedy closed her eyes tight and grunted desperately through her gag. Her tense body eventually went limp in submission.

After Joseph had defeated her spirit to resist, he stood up and pulled his satchel closer so that he could find an incense burner at the bottom of the bag. He pulled out a long leather strap with a brass boat-shaped incense burner attached. He then meticulously went about placing a large cone-shaped piece of incense inside the boat and patiently ignited it with a disposable lighter.

While he swung the smoking incense over her naked body, he recited Psalms 50:

"The mighty God, even the LORD, hath spoken, and called the earth from the rising of the sun unto the going down thereof. Out of Zion, the perfection of beauty, God hath shined. Our God shall come, and shall not keep silence – a fire shall devour before him, and it shall be very tempestuous round about him."

Joseph carried the incense around the bedroom, swinging the brass boat in circles so that the swirling scented smoke filled every corner of the room. Whenever he came across an extinguished candle, he also fired it up with the lighter.

Approaching the bed, he looked down into Kennedy's red-streaked, saturated eyes and finished his psalm by saying to her, "Thou givest thy mouth to evil, and thy tongue frameth deceit. But unto the wicked God saith, what hast thou to do to declare my statutes, or that thou shouldest take my covenant in thy mouth?"

When Kennedy didn't respond to his question, he placed the incense burner onto a nightstand near the head of the bed, unzipped his trousers and asked again. "Will thou take my covenant in thy mouth?"

The girl fervently shook her head in refusal, apparently content with having a sweaty handkerchief taped inside her mouth. Joseph became incensed over the teen's belligerence and reached for the brass boat. He reached into the boat with his thumb and index finger and removed the simmering ember, carefully clutching the cool base of the cone so as not to singe his delicate fingers.

Kennedy watched in fear as the man's fiery fingertips floated freely toward her waiting womb. Completing the transfer from the empty brass boat to the proverbial 'man in the boat,' Joseph used the fingers on his left hand to spread open her upper labia and locate the girl's bulbous bow.

"I will not reprove thee for thy sacrifices or thy burnt offerings, to have been continually before me," he announced just before he pressed the glowing red ash of the incense onto her clitoris, grinding it in by twisting his fingers along the base.

The girl violently arched her back and let loose a muffled screammmmmmmm, but Joseph managed to maintain his position and continue to extinguish the incense into her sensitive skin. The perfume-like smoke from the dying ember, mixed with the fragrant aroma of inflamed female flesh, was both pleasing and invigorating to Joseph, as it would be to any man.

When the exhausted girl's body crumpled back onto the bed, Joseph removed his hands from between her legs and tossed the blunt to the floor. He reached again for the leather-strapped incense burner. The brass boat fit perfectly in his right palm.

With little time to recover from the initial assault, Kennedy soon began to feel the stinging strikes of the leather strap across her breasts. She instinctively tried to twist her torso away from the blistering blows, but the man always seemed to find his target.

He continued to viciously whip her defenseless breasts until the bright red welts mixed in with the deep green tattoos, causing the tops of her tits to take on an eerie fluorescent yellow glow. The punished pentacles flashed and flickered under the man's relentless lashing.

Flailing her chest back and forth in sync with the incessant slashes of the strap, the girl felt like her breasts would erupt into flames at any moment. She gasped for breath in order to remain conscious, but could only obtain limited oxygen through her nose.

"Now will thou take my covenant in thy mouth?" he yelled between strikes.

Fading in and out of consciousness, the girl still managed to nod to the man with the hope that he would provide her mercy if she did what he desired. The next sting she felt was across her face as Joseph tore the duct tape from her mouth.

Kennedy managed one small gasp of breath through her mouth in the few seconds that it took the man to remove the soaked handkerchief and insert his enormous engorged cock. He had his right hand firmly behind her neck, grasping a large lock of hair, as he forced her head toward him. She felt her tethered left arm stretching painfully behind her as the tortured joint strained within her shoulder socket.

Regardless of the painful position, she resolved herself to satisfy the man who seemed ready to kill her at any moment. She wrapped her tongue around the invading shaft and worked the cock for all she was worth.

Pumping his pink pole deep into the young girl's throat, Joseph began a deprecatory exorcism prayer, reading from a tattered book held in his left hand and maintaining a perfect rhythm between his spoken words and his unspeakable thrusts:

"O God, creator and defender of the human race, look upon this Your servant, whom You did make in Your own image and call to share in Your glory. Hear, holy Father, the cry of the Church suppliant – let not Your child be possessed by the father of lies; let not Your servant, whom Christ has redeemed by His blood, to be held in the captivity of the devil; let not a temple of Your Spirit be inhabited by the unclean spirit. Hear, O merciful God, the prayers of the blessed Virgin Mary, whose Son, dying upon the Cross, crushed the head of the serpent of old and entrusted all people to His mother as sons and daughters – let the light of truth shine upon this Your servant, let the joy of peace enter into her, let the Spirit of holiness possess her, and by inhabiting her render her serene and pure. Hear, O Lord, the supplication of blessed Michael the Archangel and of all the Angels ministering unto You – God of hosts, drive back the force of the devil; God of truth and favor, remove his deceitful wiles; God of freedom and grace, break the bonds of iniquity. Hear, O God, lover of man's salvation, free this servant from every alien power."

Kennedy tried to bring him to orgasm before he finished his oral dissertation, believing that it would save her from further abuse, but she could not quite get the job done. Moments after she felt him withdraw from her mouth, she watched as he dropped his trousers to the floor and jumped onto the bed between her legs.

Balanced on his bare knees in front of her, with his huge erect cock pointing directly at her, Joseph maintained his priestly appearance by keeping on his neatly-pressed black shirt and bleached white collar band. He also kept his promise to the girl's mother by reaching into a shirt pocket and presenting her with the Rosary.

"After your mom helped tie you to the bed, she asked me to give you these anal love beads to enhance your sexual experience," he explained. "Make sure you say a Hail Mary after each bead."

He slowly fed the rough, dry, plastic beads one by one into her tight asshole, causing the girl's face to wince in pain as the sharp edges cut into her delicate flesh. Joseph had to apply more and more pressure with the insertion of each bead as her ass became more and more congested with the trinkets.

Once the entire string of beads was fully embedded, only the metal crucifix dangled against her ass cheeks. Kennedy moved her hips in agony as the prayer beads continued to bite into her inner sanctuary.

The girl's sensuous movements aroused Joseph even more as his eyes followed her gyrating hips up to meet her twisted, twitching face. He curiously observed her fluctuating face as it seemed to change composure from invaded innocence to harrowing hatred. But the transfiguration didn't stop him from violating her in the traditional submissionary position.

Beneath a furrowed brow, her pupils flared and her nostrils dilated, and her mouth growled, "Did you know lay people may not say any of the prayers of exorcism?"

"The only person getting laid around here is you, sweetie," Joseph answered as he continued to pound away at her pussy, removing his hand momentarily from the mattress in order to slap Kennedy across the face.

"You're nothing but amateur filmmakers who can't even get a wedding gig," she snarled.

"Shut up, bitch, what the fuck do you know?!" Joseph screamed, giving her another back hand.

Joseph couldn't remember the last time his cock felt so rigid. The pressure rising in his balls caused him to fuck her more furiously, straining for a release which he knew would come at any moment. He also felt the girl's body tense up like she was ready to burst into orgasm.

"Ne' aknöhsút tkanôke' ne Wátsí... Ne' aknöhsút tkanôke' ne Wátsí... Ne' aknöhsút tkanôke' ne Wátsí!"

Joseph suddenly sat up on his knees, surrounded by her outstretched legs, and began swiftly stroking his pulsing cock with his right hand. He also grabbed the end of the Rosary with his left hand and started tugging the embedded beads from her behind.

The desired cum shot rained down like lava upon the girl's stomach. After each spasm of sperm shot from the tip of his dick, Joseph commanded, "The power of Christ compels you! The power of Christ compels you! The power of Christ compels you!"

The ejaculate sizzled as it landed on the girl's inverted crucifix tattoo, causing steam to rise from the wounds. "It burns! It burns!" she screamed, yanking at her bonds with renewed vigor and vitriol.

The adrenalin rushing through the girl's panicked person proved too much for the fragile fabric tied to her left ankle and it suddenly snapped apart, freeing her leg. Joseph was still holding his pulsating prick when his forehead was met with a crippling kick.

The ball of her heel sent Joseph tumbling backward off the bed and he hit the floor hard, smacking the back of his head and ensuring his unconsciousness. Then the light bulb in the ceiling burst and the candles simultaneously went out, throwing the room into demonic darkness.

Theodore now found himself functionally alone in a barricaded room with someone or something that had more power in her left leg than he had in his entire being. Then he remembered the light that was mounted on his camera, which he was able to flick on.

The beam flashed across the girl on the bed and he caught a glimpse of her smiling at him. "Hello, Youseff," she hauntingly sang. "Put your toy down and come visit me."

31

The stocky man was shaking as he placed the camera on a dresser, positioning it so that the light continued to shine in the direction of the bed.

"How do you know my name?" he asked as he cautiously approached the girl.

"I know many secrets. Untie me and I'll tell you some."

Youseff's foot brushed against the small prayer book, which his brother had been reading from earlier. He quickly stooped over and picked it up, but tried to hide it behind his back. Even though he felt powerless against the girl, perhaps there was something in the book which could help him.

"Throw away the book, Youseff. It'll do you no good."

He ignored her and brought the book around in front of him so that he could skim through the pages. The girl growled and gnashed her teeth upon seeing him open the book.

"Please put the book down, Youseff! Look at me instead! Do you like my sexy body, Youseff? You can have it however you want, just like your brother. Oh, Youseff, my pussy's so hot and wet and tight. Don't you want to fuck me, Youseff? Please fuck me. I need your cock deep inside my cunt."

Youseff found a couple of pages where the corners had been bent down. He recognized the text on the first bent page as the words which his brother was reading earlier. The other bent page had the title "Imperative Prayer" at the top.

He cleared his throat and began reading:

"I adjure you, Satan, enemy of man's salvation, acknowledge the justice and goodness of God the Father, who by just judgment has damned your pride and envy – depart from this servant of God, whom the Lord has made in His own image, adorned with His gifts, and has mercifully adopted as His child."

"Be quiet, heathen, you don't even believe the words you're reading. This is Heresy! God will strike you down for this, Youseff!"

"I adjure you, Satan, prince of this world, acknowledge the power and strength of Jesus Christ, who conquered you in the desert, overcame you in the garden, despoiled you on the Cross, and rising from the tomb, transferred your victims to the kingdom of light."

"Please, Youseff, you're hurting me. Haven't I been hurt enough? Your brother really hurt me bad. Let me go now and I promise I won't say anything to anyone. I'll even be your girlfriend. Do you want me to be your girlfriend, Youseff?"

The girl struggled to break her other bonds, but with one leg free, she had no leverage and felt her energy draining from her body. She felt so tired, exhausted.

"I adjure you, Satan, deceiver of the human race, acknowledge the Spirit of truth and grace, who repels your snares and confounds your lies – depart from this creature of God, whom He has signed by the heavenly seal; withdraw from this girl whom God has made a holy temple by a spiritual unction."

"I'm not listening," she called out, turning her head away. "NA-NA- NA-NA- NA-NA- NA-NA- NA..."

"Leave, therefore, Satan, in the name of the Father and of the Son and of the Holy Spirit; leave through the faith and the prayer of the Church; leave through the sign of the holy Cross of our Lord Jesus Christ, who lives and reigns forever and ever. Amen!"

Youseff lowered his head, clutched the book between his palms, closed his eyes, and whispered, "I believe."

"NO!!! GODAMMIT!!! NOOO!!!" screamed the girl so loud that the window panes and door shook. Then she was silent. The whole room was deafening silent.

Kennedy wept.

Youseff looked upon her like she was his daughter and he felt the need to protect her. The stoles wrapped around the limbs of the heaving child now seemed excruciatingly cruel. He immediately worked on untying the knots and releasing her arms and leg. She quickly curled up in a fetal position and he responded by pulling the blanket and sheet from underneath her, and then wrapping the covers up over her naked body.

He heard the knob on the bedroom door rattling and realized that her mother must have heard the girl scream. He quickly gathered the stoles, incense burner and prayer book and stuffed them into the satchel. "I'm coming, Mrs. Schmulbach!"

Youseff quickly grabbed his brother's trousers and shoes from the floor and carried them over to his unconscious sibling. He struggled at first to get the pants on, but forced the trousers over his brother's limp legs and hips as soon as he heard Mrs. Schmulbach trying to break down the door. "I'm coming, Mrs. Schmulbach!"

Youseff dashed to the door and removed the chair from under the knob. Mrs. Schmulbach raced into the bedroom as soon as the door opened, almost knocking Youseff down. Light from the hall bathed the room in warmth.

"Kennedy, honey, mommy's here!"

As the two women embraced on the bed, Youseff went over to the foot of the bed where his brother was still sprawled out on the floor. He knelt down and began shaking his brother's shoulders. "Wake up, brother, wake up."

As the pseudo-priest began mumbling incoherently, Youseff heard Kennedy telling her mother how the short man had saved her. "The short man, mommy, he's the one who chased the evil away," she said in between sobs.

"Just rest dear, don't worry about it. Everything's okay. Mommy's here."

Youseff worked on getting his brother to sit up. "Come on, let me help you up. We've got to get out of here," Youseff whispered into his brother's ear.

Youseff stood up and then reached down for his brother's arm, eventually pulling his brother to his feet. His brother balanced himself against the foot of the bed and looked down curiously at the mother and daughter entangled on the bed.

"I'll get your bag *and* the camera, and then you can lean on me," instructed Youseff. "Come on now, let's get out of here and leave these two alone."

Youseff helped lead his stumbling brother across the room while he carried the bag in one hand and the camera in the other. As soon as they were in the hallway,

Youseff leaned his brother against the wall, and then shut off the camera and placed it on the floor.

He reached back inside the bedroom and grabbed the door knob. "Uhh, God bless you both," he called out to the women as he began to pull the door shut. "Oh, and Mrs. Schmulbach, you may want to wash that Rosary."

Meself and Youseff John hustled down Chapline Street toward their van. As Youseff was opening the back door of the white van to load the camera, he noticed his brother circling around to the driver's side.

"You're not thinking of driving?" he asked, slamming the door shut.

"Hell yes I'm driving," Meself shot back. "It's my fucking van."

"I think you have a concussion. What if you black out?"

"Get in the van, Youseff. We need to get out of here before those bitches call the cops."

Youseff resigned himself to climb into the front passenger seat. Although he'd been told throughout his life that he and Meself were "non-identical" twins, his brother had always been the dominant one of the pair and was always ordering him around and belittling him. Their parents had died during an armed robbery of the family business while the brothers were still in middle school. The dizygotic twins spent their teen years being shuffled around foster homes throughout the Mountain State's northern Panhandle. Now they lived in a van down by the river.

"What the fuck happened back there anyway? How'd I end up on the floor?"

Meself pulled the van out onto the street without bothering to activate the turn signal or the headlights. Youseff immediately put on his seatbelt. Fortunately, traffic was light in the city at that time of the evening.

"She kicked you. She got her foot loose and she kicked you in the head. I got it all on video."

"You damn well better have gotten it all on video. That was some pretty sweet action up there. Our customer will be very pleased."

Meself turned down Eleventh Street until he reached Main Street, and then made a quick left just as the traffic signal was turning red. Youseff knew it was futile to ask his brother to slow down. He thought he saw someone or something trying to cross the street at the crosswalk, but only heard a dull thump coming from outside the driver's side of the van.

"What was that?!"

"What was what?"

"Did you just hit something?!" asked Youseff, unsuccessfully trying to look in the side mirror.

"Hell no, I didn't hit nothin'. Just chill out and quit being so damn paranoid."

Youseff twisted around in his seat to look out one of the small windows in the back. He could see a crumpled figure in the street and it appeared to be human.

"You just hit someone, Meself!"

"Bullshit."

"No really, you hit someone in the intersection. I think he's hurt."

"Would you just turn around in your seat and calm the fuck down? I'm trying to drive here, you know?"

Youseff turned back around in his seat, but didn't calm the fuck down. "I think we should go back. Maybe take the guy to the hospital."

"Are you crazy? I just got done fucking and torturing a seventeen-year-old cunt. Not to mention *your* role in the whole ordeal. But you want me to turn around and play the Good Samaritan to someone who can't look both ways before they cross the street? Hell, you're supposed to learn that when you're five years old. Besides, it's not like the guy was a friend of yours."

Youseff shook his head in disbelief and decided to recline his head against the headrest and close his eyes, hopefully shutting out the rest of his brother's lecture. The pair rode in silence until they reached Water Street.

With his eyes still closed, Youseff eventually said, "She really was possessed, you know?"

"Who? What are you talking about?"

"The girl, Kennedy, she really was possessed by something."

"Now I know you're fuckin' seeing things. That girl was faking everything except the orgasm I gave her. She's a typical little teenage brat drama queen, starved for attention from her straight-laced momma. Maybe she'll think twice about playin' possessed now that I put her through the paces."

"I'm the one who drove the evil spirit from her. I saved her," Youseff admitted, finally opening his eyes.

"I got kicked in the head, but you're the one being delusional. What the fuck do you know about demonic possession or exorcisms?"

"I know that you read the wrong prayer in the book," Youseff answered. "You read a deprecatory prayer when you should have read an imperative prayer. You can't be polite to these demons and just request that they leave a possessed body. You have to demand it."

Meself pulled the vehicle into an alley near the river trail beside 23rd Street and turned off the ignition. He looked curiously at Youseff in the dark interior of the van and sighed.

"Youseff, don't you get it? It didn't matter what I read from that stupid book. It was just a prop. I needed some kind of mumbo jumbo to read to make it look like an exorcism. But the girl wasn't possessed, so there was no evil to exorcise."

"You didn't see it because you were knocked out on the floor, but I think I got the exorcism on camera."

"Well, you can show me tomorrow. I need to get some rest. My head is fucking killing me."

Meself retired to the back of the van, but Youseff took some rags down to the river's edge to soak them. The reflected lights from the casino across the river sparkled and blinked against cold fog-covered water. He spent a half hour wiping blood off the front bumper.

The next morning, the John brothers set out to work on editing the footage from the previous day. Using the van's cigarette lighter as a power source, they hooked the video camera up to their Apple laptop and allowed the video to upload to the iMovies software.

They both sat on their respective cots in the back of the cluttered van and waited for the data to load.

"Do we want the software to stabilize any of the shaky footage?" asked Youseff when the prompt window appeared on screen.

"No, this is supposed to be gonzo style. We may not have to edit much either, since I believe you just kept the camera rolling during the bedroom scene."

"I did, but we may not want the whole interview with the mother. Plus, we'll want to pixilate her face. It'll seem more authentic if we pixilate her."

"We'll want some of the interview, just to set up the bedroom scene. Besides, her reactions to some of my questions are hilarious. Did you see her face when I asked if her daughter had had an abortion? That was a hoot."

As the men watched the footage, Youseff continued to point out the unusual shots and angles that he obtained, explaining the rationale behind each one; while Meself continued to ignore the technical aspects of the video and, instead, boast about his performance and huge cock.

At the point where Meself began fucking the girl, Youseff pointed out, "There! Did you hear that? Her voice changed when she said she knew we were film makers and not priests. How did she know that?"

"Ah, maybe because she figured that a real priest wouldn't be torturing and raping her while his partner filmed the whole thing?"

"Okay, then, what about the foreign language? Neither of us know what language that is, but it seems to come naturally to her."

"I don't know, maybe she has some obscure Rosetta Stone CD."

Youseff waited patiently until the shot where Meself shot his load. He looked over at his brother when the footage showed the steaming cum apparently burning into the girl's skin. Youseff paused the video and crooked his head to indicate that he was expecting his brother to provide an explanation of the phenomenon.

Meself acquiesced, "We should definitely do the cum shot in slow-mo."

In frustration, Youseff clicked the play button and added, "Here's the part where she kicks you the fuck out."

But more frustration followed for Youseff when the point of impact to Meself's forehead was instantaneously followed with nothing but white noise and static interference on the screen. "What the hell?!"

"Okay, so where's the part where you save the day by exorcising the evil spirit from the innocent young maiden?" jabbed Meself.

"I don't understand this," Youseff explained while staring at the blank computer screen. "After you were kicked, the lights blew out in the room and I turned on the camera light. Then I put the camera on a dresser so that it would continue filming."

"Perhaps you should have gotten a release form signed by the devil."

"Fine! Don't believe me, I don't give a shit. Just leave me alone and I'll edit this thing so you can deliver the DVD."

"Sounds like a plan," laughed Meself, "but make a few copies because we may have additional customers. I'll step out and let you do your magic."

***

"Bless me Father, for I have sinned. It has been a week since my last confession."

"Blessed is our God, at all times, now and always and forever and ever. Amen."

"Father, I came upon the girl who was possessed by the devil."

"You came upon the one who was controlled by evil forces?"

"Yes, on her stomach, Father, right after I whipped her little titties and fucked her tight twat."

"Did she suffer under your hand?"

"Greatly, Father, there was much weeping and gnashing of teeth."

"Please describe it to me."

"Her thin naked body shivered under my hands, Father, and her skin was as smooth as the silken stoles which held her legs wide open for me. Her feminine scent excited my nostrils like a freshly cut bouquet of roses, while the red blush which covered her upper chest resembled a warm sunrise on a tropical isle. She struggled, Father, god knows she struggled against her bonds, but as a female, she knew in her heart that she had to submit to the stronger male force that held her captive. The introduction of my sturdy manhood into her defenseless passageway took her breath away. She whimpered and gasped at each thrust, her forced arousal coating my cock with sweet secretions, which emboldened and hardened me beyond any sexual encounter that I had ever experienced. The offering of her succulent nectar was rewarded in kind with wave after wave after wave of my molten love juice, spraying across her tiny tummy and reaching up to her heaving breasts. She was broken, Father, broken of the insolence, disrespect and pride of a wayward soul. And she shook, oh god how she shook and cried, her bones rattling like this wooden Confessional is rattling at this very moment under your influence."

"And you recorded all this for posterity?"

"Yes, Father, and I would like to deliver a copy of the DVD recording for the Church archives. I'll also be returning the uniforms and props you so graciously allowed me to borrow."

"That's very thoughtful of you. I assure you that the DVD will be studied thoroughly and put to good use."

"There were, of course, additional production expenditures associated with the recording."

"Yes, yes, I believe there are sufficient funds in our educational endowment that should more than cover your expenses. You've provided a great service to this institution and I am sure I'll be quite pleased with the end product."

"Yes, I'm most certain you'll be pleased by the outcome."

Later that evening, Meself angled the van off Main Street and drove deep into the back of the desolate parking lot of the Downtown Inn. Meself told Youseff that he had found a potential financier for their first full length adult film and wanted to drop off a copy of the "*Sexorcist.*"

"I thought we were gonna do my zombie flick?"

"No we ain't doin' no damn zombie flick," answered Meself. "At least not right now, anyway. Porn is where the money is. If we can get some successful porn titles under our belt, we should have the funds to branch out to the more mainstream stuff."

"Whatever. Who are we meeting?"

"You mean, who am *I* meeting? Because you're going to let me do the talking."

"Okay. Who are *you* meeting?"

"All I know is that he's called the Black Hand and he has connections to the mob. He took over the Wheeling syndicate after the Hankish family was out of the picture. He runs this place next door called the Serpents Club."

"The Black Hand? Are you serious?"

"Yes, I'm serious, so don't say anything that could fuck this up, Youseff."

"What do we call him? Mr. Hand? Or how's that going to look in the credits? Executive Producer: Black Hand."

Meself glared at his brother. "You're going to fuck this up, aren't you?"

"No. No, I'm not going to fuck anything up."

"Yes, you are. You're going to walk in there and say something stupid like, 'Hello, Mr. Hand, can I just call you Black' or some such shit. Maybe you ought to just wait in the fucking van and let me go in by myself. That way you won't fuck anything up."

"I told you, I won't fuck anything up. He needs to meet me, since I'm the cinematographer and editor. I'm your right hand man...even though I'm not black."

Meself glared.

"Get it? Right hand man and not Black Hand man?

Meself glared. "You're going to fuck this up, aren't you?"

"No, I'm not going to fuck this up."

"You better not. I'm not kidding. Don't forget, I know how to run that fucking camera and I can edit footage too."

"I know, I know, I'm not going to fuck it up."

The men got out of the van, dressed in their usual jeans and coats, and walked through some shrubbery to gain access to the Greater Wheeling River Trail, which runs along the east bank of the Ohio River. The trail, of course, was deserted since it was a colder than average Fall evening, but the John brothers did not have far to walk.

A smaller unpaved path led to a private parking lot tucked in behind a squarish two-floor red brick building with tan ornately-framed windows symmetrically adorning each side, six per wall unless there was a door. The windows all had dark curtains, ensuring the privacy of the activities taking place within. There were no signs on the building, thus leading the casual observer to conclude that it must be a private residence.

Meself walked onto the back deck and knocked on a solid white door. He whispered to his brother, "My

45

contact said no one ever enters through the front Main Street entrance."

The door cracked open and a strong female voice asked, "Who are you and what do you want?"

"My name is Meself John and I'm here with my brother, Youseff. We're here to see the Black Hand."

She added, "The Black Hand? Are you serious?"

"Yes, I'm serious. We have an appointment."

"With the Black Hand?"

"Yes, with the Black Hand."

"Well, I can't let you in without seeing some form of I.D."

"I assure you, we're both twenty-one."

"That's nice, but I can't let you in without seeing some form of I.D."

Each man retrieved his driver's license and thrust it, one at a time, through the cracked opening of the door. Eventually, the door opened wide enough to allow for entry and it revealed a tall, wiry, bald-headed female standing just inside the threshold. The hairless young woman wore a skin-tight green dress, which skirted off just below her ass cheeks, and turquoise heels. Her legs were covered in black, scale-like, eelnet hose.

She motioned for them to enter and they followed her into the dimly lit club. There were no interior walls on the first floor, only some support beams. The woman took her regular place behind the bar, while the men found empty bar stools on the opposite side. Most of the other anonymous patrons were seated at small tables scattered around the interior.

A small stage was situated adjacent to the bar and featured a brass pole attached to the floor and ceiling. The only lights in the room were multi-colored stage lights and spotlights, which primarily illuminated a pale well-proportioned exotic dancer (i.e., stripper). Bad eighties arena-style rock music blared from speakers strategically configured on the walls around the room.

Avoiding eye contact with her new customers, the tall woman asked, "Would you gentlemen like something to drink?"

Meself had been ignoring the stripper on stage, concentrating his attention on the much younger bartender, and finally noticing that she also had no eye brows.

"Do you have any Iron City?"

"Yeah, in bottles. Does your brother want the same?"

With a straight face, Youseff said, "I'll have a Slippery Bald Beaver."

Meself retorted, "You'll have an Iron City and like it."

"Sorry," smirked the bartender, "I'm all out of strawberry juice."

"An Iron City will be fine then."

As soon as the young woman stepped away, Meself chastised, "You do plan to fuck this up, don't you?"

"No, I mean, I saw the Bailey's Irish Cream on the shelf there and I thought I'd try a mixed drink…"

"Since when do you order mixed drinks? You need to just sit there and be quiet. Dammit, I know you're gonna fuck this up!"

When the bartender came back with the bottles, Meself thanked her, adding, "And I want to apologize for my brother. He's a little slow, if you know what I mean."

Youseff lowered his head, trying to control a rising anger. Youseff absolutely despised Meself when he tried to embarrass him in front of girls. He thought he had caught a glimpse of the bartender smiling at him when he first sat down and had planned on joking with her a bit. But Meself appeared intent on ruining that.

"Tell me something," Meself said, changing the subject and pushing a ten-dollar bill toward the bartender. "Why's there no chairs up against the stage? The girls won't get many tips like that... By the way, keep the change."

The young woman glanced over to the stage, silently acknowledging his reference, and then explained, "The dancers don't work for tips. They work at the behest of the Black Hand."

"Ah ha! So you do know the Black Hand!"

"I never said I didn't. He runs this place. I work here. So I must know him. But I'm not going to broadcast that to every Tom, Dick and Ahmed who come banging at the back door."

"Point taken," Meself replied as the woman strutted to the other end of the bar.

Nursing their beers, Meself and Youseff silently sat through the shimmy n' shake set of the featured pole-prancer, including "*Photograph*" by Def Leppard and "*She's a Beauty*" by the Tubes. Meself hoped the Black Hand would soon make an appearance; otherwise the monotone music was going to worm itself deep inside his psyche and get stuck on auto replay for the next few days.

The thick thuds of heavy shoes stomping down wooden stairs were eventually heard over the music and took everyone's attention away from the gyrating joystick teaser. A large sixtyish well-dressed man, weighing at least 300 pounds, appeared around the corner of the staircase. The suit he wore was all black, which matched everything from his shiny leather shoes up to his slick greasy hair. Oh yeah, this guy was Italian all right.

As the old fat man walked past the stage, the stripper genuflected and waited for the man's hand to be presented in front of her lowered head. When she saw the bright yellow gold ring on his pinky finger, she quickly kissed the jewelry and waited for him to pass before continuing with her routine.

He approached the bar and leaned over to speak to the bartender, making sure no one else could hear. "Is these the fellas who want to see me?"

"Yeah, but I don't trust them. I think you ought to toss them the fuck out."

"Not 'til I hear what they have to say, my dear."

Meself and Youseff watched the couple converse from the other end of the bar. Meself wondered whether the man was getting to fuck the sweet young thing. Of course, he himself wouldn't fuck the girl unless she put on some kind of wig, preferably blonde, on her barren wasteland of a head.

After a few minutes, the man made his way over to the brothers and invited them to take their beers over to an empty table near the back of the room. He also yelled to the bartender to bring them two more bottles.

As soon as the three men sat down, the woman was right at the table with the fresh beers.

"Did you want something, sir?"

"Yeah, sweetheart," the man answered. "Bring me a Bald Pussy!"

The man burst out laughing and the girl followed his lead. Before walking away, she said, "That's a good one, sir! I'll whip one up for you right away!"

Youseff mumbled, "What the fuck?" while Meself kicked him under the table.

"Did you get that boys? I ordered a Bald Pussy from a bald bartender!"

"Yeah, yeah, we get it, but I wonder if her pussy really is bald."

"I wouldn't know, she only works here because I owed her daddy a favor."

"If you don't mind my asking," Meself said, leaning closer to the man. "Is she even old enough to be tending bar?"

"This ain't the Waves at Wheeling Peninsula. This is a private club and I make the rules."

"Point taken."

The bartender soon returned with a large fruit colored concoction and placed the glass on a napkin in front of the man. "One melon liqueur and vodka mix, sir."

"Thank you dear, but how'd you know I was a melon licker?"

Again the duo broke out laughing. "Well, I need to get back to the bar now," she concluded, making sure she didn't look at either Meself or Youseff as she slithered away.

The man noticed how she blew off the two brothers. "She don't like you boys, does she?"

"Maybe she just doesn't like strangers. She seemed suspicious of us when we knocked."

"Well, I hope you didn't try hittin' on her, 'cause she don't like guys. She lets me joke around with her because I'm a friend of the family."

"Plus she works for you," Meself suggested.

"Yeah, that too, I suppose... Speakin' of working for me, I understand you have a business proposition."

Meself reached inside his coat to produce a DVD in a white paper sleeve, while Youseff resigned himself to watching the stripper so he wouldn't be accused of fucking anything up.

"This, sir, is an example of JB Video Arcade's work. This was a production privately commissioned by our mutual friend, Vince Frobass. Obviously, discretion is of utmost importance, but Vinny did give me permission to burn you a personal copy."

"Well, thank you, Mr. John, I have no problem keeping my business dealings discreet. I also see that your brother there has no problem keeping quiet when it comes to business. He doesn't say much, does he?"

"You'll have to forgive my brother. It's not that he's uninterested in our business. It's just that he is, well, my brother happens to be mildly retarded."

Youseff took his eyes off the stripper momentarily in order to turn his head and grimace toward his brother. "Don't go there, brother," he warned.

"He speaks!" announced the man with a boisterous guffaw.

"Yes," continued Meself anyway. "We are actually twins, by the way, but it seems my brother Youseff was deprived of some oxygen during the pregnancy. Our mother actually had a sonogram showing me in the womb with my little hands strangling Youseff's throat."

Youseff just shook his over-heated head, gulped down some cold beer, and went back to watching the strip show. The prospect of 'fucking everything up' was becoming more and more appealing to Youseff.

The man observed the brothers closely. "But yet you want me to invest in a project with you and your retarded brother? This is supposed to look like a sound investment for me?"

"Oh don't worry about that. Youseff does the camera work on our videos and he's excellent. You've heard how some retards tend to be good at one specific thing, like playing the piano or counting cards? Well, Youseff's hidden talent is cinematography."

"An idiot savant of the cinema?" suggested the man.

"That's it," Youseff countered, slamming his bottle down on the table and standing up. "I am out of here. I'll be waiting in the van."

As Youseff stormed off toward the back door, the man added, "Your brother's a bit touchy, isn't he?"

"Yes, he's been that way ever since our parents died. They died while we were still kids and he's sort of always been my responsibility."

"That's very admirable of you. Family is very important. You've got to look out for each other."

"Well, that's sort of why I'd like to see our film company be successful and I believe if we had the funding to make a full length adult movie, we'd be able to branch out into other genres. For instance, Youseff would like to make a horror film some day."

"So tell me about this adult film project you are proposing."

"Okay, the working title is '*The Manacled*' and it takes place inside a women's prison. Women prison movies are always cult favorites and I plan on kicking it up a notch. You know, with the male guards fucking the prisoners and butch dyke inmates raping the new girls. I've even got a full script, if you're interested in seeing it."

"Are you going to have to build sets and buy a lot of prison type props?"

"No not at all. That's the great thing about this idea. We've got the perfect location right down the road in Moundsville – the former West Virginia State Penitentiary. Have you ever toured that place? It's fucking awesome."

"Sorry, but I have no interest getting anywhere near a penitentiary – even if it is shut down. But I'm curious to know why you think the management at the prison would allow you to film a porno on the grounds. Don't you think the tourists will be a little put off when they walk past a couple of chicks chowing down on each other's cunt meat?"

"That won't be a problem either. You see, the prison rents out the property all the time to these nutty paranormal investigators or ghost hunters. They come in with a camera crew and all this pseudo-sci-fi equipment and basically have the run of the place for an entire night. Thus, I'll just call up the prison and tell them that I'm interested in filming a paranormal documentary. They won't even have a clue what we're really doing."

"Sounds plausible, I suppose. So your budget would include renting out the prison for one night, hiring the actors, and maybe some costumes and incidental props. And catering, you may require catering."

"We'll also need to rent some additional lighting and sound equipment, since what we have on hand at our storage locker is inadequate for this kind of production."

The man looked down at his glass, took a sip, swished the liquid around briefly in his mouth, and swallowed. He made eye contact with Meself.

"Okay, assuming this DVD you've given me is acceptable from a production standpoint, I could probably put up enough money to make the movie happen, but it would have to be under my strict terms."

"Name 'em."

"All right, all the initial profits from the end product would go directly to me, until my initial investment is paid off. After that point, we would split all profits fifty-fifty. The first thing I will need from you is a detailed, itemized budget, breaking down all expected expenses. I'll also want a personal representative on hand during the production to ensure that my investment is secure and that you're delivering on the product as described."

"That sounds reasonable. We'll designate the person of your choosing as a producer – even recognize him in the credits as such if he wants."

"Well, it probably won't be a *he*; it'll probably be my assistant, Kay."

"That's fine, I don't have a problem with that."

"That's good, because I don't like problems."

Both men finished their drinks and looked over at the stripper going through her motions to the tune of Whitesnake's "*Slide It In*."

"There's one other thing," the man mumbled, keeping his eyes focused on the stripper. "I want to sit in on the auditions."

"I hadn't given much thought to auditions. I was just about to ask if any of your dancers would be interested in performing."

"No, you can't have any of my girls, but I can give you the web address that I use to find local talent. It's an adult modeling site for girls who are willing to work cheap. It's called twobitwhores dot com."

"That sounds interesting. I'll definitely check it out."

"I own the Mary Isabella Apartments next door. You can use that location for the auditions, since the building is being renovated and no one should be in there. But I'd like you to leave your brother at home for the auditions. No offense, but I'd like just you and me to be there."

"No offense taken. We'll just mount the camera on a tripod and let it roll."

"I'll also be needing a DVD of the screen tests. You can consider it as a...privately-commissioned project for me."

"In that case, I guess I'll be killing two birds with one stone."

***

For the better part of a week, Meself worked tirelessly on the project, polishing the script, creating a budget, checking on the costs of renting equipment and on leasing the prison. He figured that he could get away with having four porn actresses, as long as they were willing to perform all the odd sex scenes that he envisioned. Youseff wasted his time writing zombie fiction.

Meself also found the www.twobitwhores.com website to be useful, especially the feature that allowed him to search for so-called models within thirty miles of downtown Wheeling. Even with the elimination of all the skanky-looking sluts, Meself was still able to send out numerous emails to local women advertising on the site who showed potential. Of course, the auditions would reveal whether they'd be willing not only to show their potentials, but allow Meself to abuse and ravish their potentials.

Of the girls who responded favorably to the audition offering, he was able to set up eight interviews at one hour intervals on a day that the Black Hand was available. He was happy with the final selection of interviewees, because the final four would certainly represent his concept of having an "international cast."

On the designated day, Meself showed up early at the Mary Isabella Apartments to set up the equipment in the first floor apartment, which the Black Hand had reserved for the auditions. In order to look professional, Meself was dressed in one of the few business suits that he owned. Plus, he had remembered how the Black Hand was dressed in the club.

The apartment was being refurbished and Meself immediately noticed the strong musty smell of fresh white paint on the walls. The windowless living room was the largest room in the apartment and Meself chose it to conduct the interviews.

There was no furniture, but Meself found three folding chairs, which the painters must have been using. Thick plastic sheets still covered what appeared to be new carpeting on the floor. Meself had about a half hour to set up the tripod, camera, lighting and chairs before the first girl arrived. He gave the Black Hand a call shortly after the equipment was in place.

When the Black Hand showed up, Meself was surprised to see the old man dressed in baggy sweatpants and a raggy white sleeveless T-shirt. He was also lugging a low-backed red rattan chair through the door. He placed it beside a folding chair, which Meself had strategically placed in the middle of the room for the interviewees.

"I thought this chair would look good for the screen tests. It's rattan."

"Fine with me, boss," replied Meself as he got up from his seat to adjust the camera and light stand for the rattan chair.

The successful interviews included the following:

Joy D. Switt

Meself: Tell us about yourself.

Joy: Me? I'm twenty years old. My name is Joy, which I think is a real good name for an actress.

Meself: As in *spread the Joy*?

Joy: Gee, I guess, I never thought of it that way. Anyways, I'm a Wheeling girl, born and raised. I went to Wheeling Park High School. I was head majorette and runner-up prom queen and all that, but after I graduated I found life around Wheeling to be pretty boring and stuff. That's why I set up a profile on that modeling website.

Meself: Are you aware this is a hardcore adult film?

Joy: Yes, your email was pretty clear on that.

Meself: Then why are you still dressed?

Joy: Oops, sorry.

(Notes: Cute natural red head, nicely-proportioned, must work out, beautiful freckled tits, tight ass, she'd be good for the American role).

Meself: The film takes place in a women's prison, so do you have any problem with S&M, bondage, lesbian sex or even anal sex?

Joy: As long as there's no blood. I faint dead away if I even get a paper cut. But other than that, I'm open for pretty much anything.

Meself: Do you have any experience in adult films or adult entertainment?

Joy: Well, my old boyfriend used to film me with his phone when I'd suck him off, but he promised it was just for his personal use. Later, someone must have hacked into his phone 'cause it ended up getting all around school. I was almost expelled. It was so embarrassing, oh gosh.

Meself: Was that the clip you uploaded to the website?

Joy: Oh, yeah, I forgot I added that to my profile.

Meself: Do you have any food allergies or are you allergic to penicillin?

Joy: No, but remember I don't like needles.

Meself: If you were a tree, what kind would you be?

Joy: Oh my, I never thought about that. Maybe a cherry tree, since this'll be my first movie if I'm selected.

Meself: Good answer. If you're chosen for our multi-cultural cast, your character will be the so-called All-American Girl, who has made some mistakes and ends up in prison. As the new inmate, the veteran convicts will attempt to victimize you, so you'll have to earn their respect. I have a portion of the script here, which I'd like you to read for us…

Virginia Foxxx

Meself: Tell us about yourself.

Virginia: My name is Virginia Foxxx, with three X's, so you know I'm serious about this porno shit. I was born across the bridge in Steubenville, but I grew up in Weirton.

Meself: Steubenville, huh? Did you know Traci Lords is from Steubenville?

Virginia: That skinny-assed bitch? I can fuck rings around that hoe. Besides, with me, you at least know I'm legal, 'cause I'm twenty-six-fucking-years-old.

Meself: Dean Martin is also from Steubenville.

Virginia: Dean who?

Meself: Never mind. Are you aware this is a hardcore adult film?

Virginia: Hell, yeah, I know this shit is old school, hardcore, triple-x, porn!

Meself: Then why are you still dressed?

Virginia: Don't have to ask me twiced. Check this out. I got it goin' on!

(Notes: African American, got it goin' on, short, but nice bubble butt, big tits, hair cropped short and dyed a disturbing blonde color, needs her bush trimmed a bit, seems excited about the project, would work as the dyke antagonist).

Meself: The film takes place in a women's prison, so do you have any problem with S&M, bondage, lesbian sex or anal sex?

Virginia: Hell no, I do all that shit. Been there; done that. I'll go down on you right now if you want me to.

Meself: Do you have any experience in adult films or adult entertainment?

Virginia: Excuse me? You ain't never heard of '*Butt-Bangin' Beauties*' or '*Black Assed Bitches*'? They was filmed outta Pittsburgh. They sell 'em at the Tiger's Den, two for twenty-five.

Meself: Do you have any food allergies or are you allergic to penicillin?

Virginia: Why's that? You ain't got no VD disease, do you?

Meself: No, we have to ask that question for insurance purposes.

Virginia: Then no, I don't have no allergies.

Meself: If you were a tree, what kind would you be?

Virginia: Tree? Is that another insurance question? Don't ask me about no tree, unless you got a limb you want to plant somewhere.

Meself: If you're chosen for our multi-cultural cast, your character will likely be the so-called tough veteran con who controls all the other girls, but ends up getting her authority challenged by a new inmate. I have a portion of the script here, which I'd like you to read for us...

Star Blaze

Meself: Tell us about yourself.

Star: I am a nineteen-year-old full-blooded Native American woman with roots which can be traced back to the Mingo Tribe that first populated this region. I grew up on the Powhatan Point Reservation, although I currently live and work in downtown Wheeling, specifically at Capo Di Tutti Capi's Gentleman's Club and Deli near Wheeling Peninsula.

Meself: Did you know that the name Wheeling is an Indian term for Place of the Skull?

Star: I am reminded of my father's tales every time I perform for the leering eyes of the white man.

Meself: You've never worked at the Serpents Club?

Black Hand: Not yet she hasn't.

Meself: Are you aware this is a hardcore adult film?

Star: Yes, I'm aware of the nature of your project.

Meself: Then why are you still dressed?

Star: I guess I was waiting for that Wheeling feeling.

(Notes: There may not even be a need to continue the audition, this girl is smoking hot, she's tall, thin, luscious black hair stretching all the way down to her scarlet ass, and the clincher has to be her albino areolas!).

Meself: The film takes place in a women's prison, so I hope to hell you don't have any problem with S&M, bondage, lesbian sex or anal sex?

Star: I've already resigned myself to a career where my body is defiled.

Meself: Do you have any experience in adult films?

Star: I was featured in a Girls Be Wild video when the company was in town for the Jesuit Spring Break Party last year. My segment was unfortunately called '*Pokeahotass*.'

Meself: Do you have any food allergies or are you allergic to penicillin?

Star: None that I know of. I am a vegetarian.

Meself: If you were a tree, what kind would you be?

Star: Got Redwood?

Meself: If you're chosen for our multi-cultural cast (and you probably will be), your character will be the loyal companion to the main convict who controls all the other inmates. Your loyalty will be tested throughout the story. I have a portion of the script here, which I'd like you to read for us…

<u>Jennie Dagmaar</u>

Meself: Tell us about yourself.

Jennie: My name is Jennie Dagmaar and I am now working as a housekeeper at the Downtown Inn. I graduated from Central Catholic, but can find no other work around here but meanie-old labor. I would like to eventually save enough money to allow me to move away from this place. My brothers and sisters all want to stay here, but I do not.

Meself: Are you aware this is a hardcore adult film?

Jennie: I will do what I have to do.

Meself: Then why are you still dressed?

Jennie: Fine.

(Notes: Latina, nice plump ass and firm titties, not much taller than the Foxxx chick, pretty and innocent looking face, light brown hair pulled back in a bun, seems slightly embarrassed, but will probably do what she's asked to do).

Meself: The film takes place in a women's prison, so do you have any problem with S&M, bondage, lesbian sex or even anal sex?

Jennie: I guess not. I'm twenty-four years old, but I've never experimented with the gay love-making.

Meself: Do you have any experience in adult films or adult entertainment?

Jennie: Well... excuse me for my emotions. I was once tricked by men who cornered me in a motel room. They offered me money to take pictures of me naked, but then they beat me up and did not pay. They said they would put the pictures or video on the Internet if I said anything.

Meself: I find it hard to believe someone would take advantage of a sweet girl like you. Sometimes I'm surprised at just how cruel people can be to one another.

Jennie: Thank you.

Meself: Do you have any food allergies or are you allergic to penicillin?

Jennie: No, sir.

Meself: If you were a tree, what kind would you be?

Jennie: A kind of tree? You mean like a Christmas Tree? Because that's what kind of tree I'd like to be. Christmas Trees make me feel happy inside.

Meself: Feliz Navidad. If you're chosen for our multi-cultural cast, your character will probably be a submissive girlfriend to one of the other prisoners. I have a portion of the script here, which I'd like you to read for us...

One of the unsuccessful interviews was the following:

Meself: Tell us about yourself.

Sei: My name is Sei Zen Zhu. I am seventeen years old, but hope to be eighteen before your movie begins.

Meself: Are you aware this is a hardcore adult film?

Sei: I am used to hard work. I worked at my parents' restaurant since I was very young.

Meself: Why are you still dressed?

Sei: I do not understand.

Meself: Please undress so we can see what you look like.

(Notes: Scrawny Asian, no tits, language barrier, may not realize what she's here for, plus she's underage!).

Meself: Sei, does anyone know you're here today, like family or friends?

Sei: No, this must be kept secret.

Meself: That's what I thought.

Black Hand: I'd like to help her with the screen test, if you don't mind.

Sei: There is a test?

Meself: I have a portion of the movie script here, which I'd like you to read for us.

The Black Hand grabbed the script and carried it over to the nude girl seated in the rattan chair. He handed the papers to her and stood behind the chair while the girl studied the high-lighted lines. She suddenly gasped, either from the graphic nature of the lines or from the straight razor, which was placed at the base of her throat.

"Look into the camera, sweetheart, and show us your best scared look," the Black Hand whispered into her ear from behind.

"I do not like this, please let me leave," she cried out.

The Black Hand grabbed a handful of hair with his left hand, pulling the girl's head back, and then dragged the razor full across her throat, severing her external jugular vein like a knife through room temperature margarine. The girl's eyes widened in horror as she felt the sharp blade encircle her throat and she instinctively brought her hands up to grasp the man's wrist.

"Holy fucking shit!" screamed Meself, jumping to his feet.

The girl vainly tried to cry out again, but only the gurgling of rising blood could be heard emanating from her open mouth – her tongue flapping fervently inside. As soon as the man's hand with the razor was removed from her neck, she desperately grasped at her gaping throat, blood seeping out between her dainty fingers.

"What the fuck are you doing?" demanded Meself, approaching the chair.

"Stand back boy!" yelled the Black Hand as he pulled back farther on the girl's head, opening the wound up even more. "And get outta the fucking camera shot!"

Blood gushed like a geyser out of her gorge, spraying across the plastic-covered floor like a tsanguine tsunami. The girl's blood-soaked body broke out in spasms and her frightened face erupted in panicked tics and twitches. She began coughing and choking, spurting blood from her mouth straight into the air, like a colored casino fountain, and striking the freshly-painted ceiling.

The Black Hand jumped back, trying his best not to get into the Splash Zone. "Let's watch," he announced proudly, "and see whether she dies of blood loss, choking on her own blood or suffocation, since there's no air entering her lungs!"

Her convulsing, pulsating, blood-spewing body fell from the chair onto the slippery plastic. The flailing of her arms and legs resembled the movements of a drowning child who had stumbled into a negligent neighbor's unprotected pool.

"Look at her go, Meself! Look at her go!"

Meself didn't know how to react. He just stood to the side and watched the life drain out of the naked girl. Eventually the girl stopped moving. The smell of spilled blood permeated the room and made Meself sick to his stomach. He glanced around the bloodied room, including the dripping ceiling, and then focused on the grinning evil figure of the Black Hand.

"What do we do now?"

"Do not worry, Mr. John. I shall wrap the girl up in the plastic and carry her upstairs to a vacant room. I'll bury her when I have time."

"Look at this mess though. We've only got about a half hour before the arrival of Jennie Dagmaar!"

***

Ascending like an unscalable sandstone volcano, carved from the midst of the paradisiacal residential oasis known as Moundsville, is the imposing nineteen-acre expanse of the West Virginia State Penitentiary.

Built by convicts in 1866 for their own pending incarceration, the West Virginia State Penitentiary encompasses four city blocks with its four-foot thick hand-chiseled sandstone walls, rising twenty-four feet into the sky; its ominous castellated parapet; and its half-dozen fortified guard turrets. It remains the only true castle edifice in Founding Father Francis Harrison Pierpont's storybook land called West 'By God' Virginia, but there were never any princes or princesses prancing about its palisade – only kingpins, pen queens and an assortment of sordid peasantry.

Directly across from the pedestrian entrance on Jefferson Avenue is a far more ancient tomb, where the city got its name, specifically the Grave Creek Mound; where dead Indian upon dead Indian upon dead Indian were piled on top of one another and burned over the course of a century, creating one ominous sixty-nine-foot high pile of fertilized earth. Today it's a really neat park and you can walk up to the top and sit there and stuff.

"Jinkies! I don't know what's creepier, the prison or that mound across the street," observed Youseff, hoping to create some semblance of conversation with his brother as they parked the overloaded van in the penitentiary's visitor lot on the afternoon of the shoot.

"Shut the fuck up, Youseff," the brother snapped, staring straight ahead through the dusty windshield at the gray stone wall in front of the van. "We've gotta take this shit seriously. If you saw what I saw during the auditions, then you'd know we'd better not screw this thing up. This Black Hand guy doesn't fool around."

"So, what did ya see? You kept all this audition stuff to yourself, even the editing."

"You don't want to know."

"I'm the cameraman, the lighting guy, the sound guy and all the other technical roles for this film, so maybe I do want to know."

"You don't want to know."

"All right, then I don't want to know. Let's just get the equipment unloaded."

But Meself didn't budge.

"The last couple girls," he confessed, shaking his head but still refusing to look at his brother. "The last couple of girls he interviewed, he asked them directly if they'd ever starred in a snuff film before."

"How'd they answer?"

Meself finally turned to his brother. "What do mean, 'How'd they answer'? Of course, they answered no."

"I guess you can't really build a career around starring in snuff films."

"Never mind, you just don't get it. We need to unload."

It was the day before Thanksgiving, but the temperatures were still on the mild side, hovering in the mid-fifties at night. The brothers, who were dressed in jeans and heavy sweatshirts, had the foresight to rent an industrial space heater since the so-called talent was going to be naked a lot of the time and there were no working furnaces inside the prison.

Speaking of the talent, the girls happened to appear onsite just after the boys had finished hauling all the equipment into the visitor's lobby of the prison. A former prison guard, who now served as a tour guide for the facility, was very cordial to the men while they waited for the rest of the cast to show up, but became more and more suspicious as the women began straggling in, dressed provocatively out of season, and strutting about like prima donnas.

"Hey, wait a second; this isn't one of them MTV reality shows is it? Because MTV was banned from the premises after they tore the place up last time."

"No, no, like I said, we're a small Wheeling, West Virginia production company here to do a paranormal documentary," reiterated Meself. "We got nuthin' to do with MTV or any other pseudo reality show. In fact, the Moundsville Economic Development Committee was very enthusiastic about having a local company film here."

The old guard took a particular interest in Star Blaze, who was leaning seductively over a glass case representing the tour's gift shop, her long black hair draping over her back. "Are you sure? Because I'm thinking I saw that squaw dancing at a local club."

Meself, who was caught off guard by the old guard's off-hand remark, looked sheepishly to his brother for assistance.

"You mean Doctor Half Moon?" Youseff jumped in. "She's a biology professor at WVU and she heads up the Mountaineer Paranormal Club. Most of the young ladies here are members of the club."

"Is that right? Well, she sure likes to show off her ass cheeks in that loin cloth thingy she's wearing."

"It's a cultural thing, plus you know how liberal the university is. It's a wonder they wear clothes at all in that place."

"Well, none of these WVU students better be burnin' any couches or anything else tonight, unless you want to lose your security deposit."

"Point taken," Meself added.

Once the Black Hand's bald-headed assistant, Kay, slithered into the lobby in her black business suit, featuring a long black skirt, Meself indicated to the guard that everyone from the cast and crew appeared to be in attendance. The guard then called everyone together in the center of the room.

"Welcome to the West Virginia State Penitentiary. You are standing in the area where the normal tours begin and end, but y'all have signed up for the Private Paranormal Investigation or PPI for short. This lobby area was once used to screen family members who came to the prison to visit some of the more dangerous inmates. To your left, under the machine gun cage, is the area where the family members sat for their visits with the inmates, which, as you can see, were separated by glass partitions.

"Behind me is the door where you will enter into the Main Corridor to begin your PPI. You are very fortunate to start your PPI early, since tomorrow is a holiday. Usually the PPIs start between twenty-three and twenty-four hundred hours, but I will still come by tomorrow morning to dismiss y'all and do a quick inspection of the grounds. As y'all should have read on the Paranormal License Application and Agreement Form, *which each of you signed*, you cannot take away

71

anything from the property and you cannot leave anything behind. You also cannot damage the property or change it in any way. Mr. John has paid eight hundred dollars for this opportunity, plus he put up a hundred and fifty dollar security deposit, but you are still each responsible for any type of damage done to this facility. This place is slowly crumbling apart on its own and it doesn't need any additional help from you.

"Okay, now that the formalities are out of the way, I usually tell the PPI groups about some of the paranormal activities that have been witnessed here over the years. One of the most popular apparitions is that of Ardie Waugh, who was once a maintenance man for the prison back in the seventies. But Ardie got a little too close to the inmate population and soon began informing on their illicit activities to the guards. When Ardie heard that a pistol had been smuggled into the facility, a couple of his inmate buddies were afraid he'd squeal, so Ardie was savagely tortured and murdered in the boiler room. The prison report states that the inmates first cut off Ardie's fingers and toes with a fire axe, and eventually chopped off his head. Visitors continue to report sightings of Ardie's ghost, especially in the bathroom areas.

"Red Snider is another spirit, who is said to still haunt the prison. Red was convicted of killing his parents, cutting up their bodies and hiding the dismembered pieces under his bed. Everyone avoided Red because he was a psychotic, but one day a fellow inmate rushed into his cell as soon as the guards opened the slammer bar. Red got stabbed thirty-seven times with a shank, causing his cell to take on the same crimson color as his name.

"Then there's the strange case of Anvil Adkins, whose noose malfunctioned during his execution and he ended up falling through the trap door of the gallows and busting his head open on the pavement. But the guards scooped up his unconscious body, carried him back up the thirteen steps of the gallows and hung him again. Some say he still *hangs around* the area where the gallows once stood..."

Kay sharply clapped her hands twice, but it wasn't out of appreciation for the guard's performance. "Let's just cut out the ghost mumbo-jumbo and get to work! Time is money people! If you wanna talk to the nice man, do it tomorrow as you're leaving."

"But I love a man in uniform," protested Virginia Foxxx.

"Love him on your own time, Foxxx. We've got a film to make."

The guard grimaced either from Kay's interruption or Virginia's confession, or both, but agreed to cut his introduction short and step aside for the cast and crew to enter the Main Corridor. "I'll just be on my way then. Y'all have my contact information if you need anything."

After the old guard took his leave, the John brothers convinced the cast to help them carry various pieces of equipment out of the lobby and into the Main Corridor. Everyone helped except Kay, of course, who carried a clipboard and pen for taking notes in short hand for the Black Hand.

The group walked to the left upon reaching the Main Corridor and began following Youseff, who had mapped out the facility using a DirectX 3-D Model of the prison, which had been set up on the Internet for Law Enforcement use only, specifically to facilitate the annual mock riot training in the facility. Youseff was leading them to the small five-by-seven foot cells comprising the North Hall, which the inmates once called "The Alamo."

***

"Midnight Sexpress" Scene – Take One

Jennie Dagmaar, playing the role of Snifki, watches from her cell as a new prisoner is brought into the block by Meself the Guard. Both Jennie, and the new prisoner, Joy Switt, are dressed in loose-fitting gray prison garb. Meself pushes Joy into the dingy cell beside Jennie, and then slams the steel door shut. Joy slowly gets up from the floor, shivering from the cold cement. Wrapping her arms across her chest, she pleads to Meself.

Lookie: Can I have a blanket? Do you think I could have a blanket? It's cold. Could I have a blanket?! A blanket?!

Guard: No, ma'am. It's too late. Maybe tomorrow. You'll still be here tomorrow, I think. You'll get it then. Goodnight.

Meself walks away as Joy sits down on the filthy cot, which is hanging precariously off the wall. She brushes some dirt off the stained sheets and begins to cry. She hears Jennie in the next cell talking to her.

Snifki: Soy una criada aquí en este establecimiento. Las mantas están en la célula tres. La puerta está abierta.

Joy walks over to the bars.

Lookie: Do you speak English?

Snifki: Your cell. It's open. Blankets are three cells down.

Joy tugs hard at the steel door and it budges a bit. She tries harder and the rusty cell door inches open just enough for her to squeeze through. She scampers along the cellblock until she locates an empty cell with some blankets folded onto the cot. She grabs the blankets and runs back to her cell, handing one to her neighbor through the bars. She then pulls her door closed and goes to bed with her blanket.

The crash of the cell door being thrown open by Meself awakens Joy from her sleep. He rushes in and places handcuffs and a blindfold on Joy, and then leads her out of the cell. They march to a common fenced area where a few metal tables are bolted to the floor. Low-hanging chain-link fence makes the small area look like an animal kennel. There is also a fenced-in shower area beside the tables. Joy stumbles blindly into one of the tables.

Guard: Lookie Jackson!

Lookie: I'm sorry about the blankets. I was cold.

Meself slaps her hard across the face, making her red hair flit through the air like a raging wild fire. He begins to beat her mercilessly with a leather razor strop, beginning just above her hips and making his way down to her thighs. She desperately tries to protect herself with her bound hands in front of her, but ends up on the floor screaming and kicking as the blows continue.

Meself violently rips her prison clothes off, leaving her naked on the cold floor. He grabs some rope and begins wrapping it around her ankles. Once her legs are bound together, Meself drags her into the shower area and ties her upside down to a faucet, which is jutting through the fence. Joy, whose head and shoulders are still touching the floor, cries and whimpers throughout the ordeal.

Meself takes out a peacock feather.

At first, the sensations are strange to the blindfolded girl and she starts curling her toes in response to the feather tickling the soles of her feet. But as the feather continues its relentless attack on her feet, she begins swinging her body back and forth against the fence wall. She is now making sounds like a Beatles album being played backward – an erotic mix of forced laughter and involuntary sobbing.

Lookie: Please stop it. Please stop. I can't take it anymore. You're killing me. Please stop!

But the torment continues and Joy's body begins to convulse, leaping off the side of the fence like a marlin fighting against the line of an angler. Meself is careful not to allow her thrashing body to interrupt his work as he continues to drive the feather deep and furiously into her reddening soles. Soon the soles of her feet match the color of her frazzled hair.

Lookie: Oh, god, please you have to stop. I can't take this. Please, please, please stop!

Meself smells the acidic scent of urine and looks down to see Joy's piss cascading down her body as if the faucet had suddenly been turned on. Joy is now drenched in her own pee as it freely flows over her breasts, around her neck and chin, and mixes with her oranging hair.

Meself continues the assault until the tap runs dry, but Joy continues to splash about in her puddle while her cries turn to deep throaty groans.

Lookie: Oh, god, I think I'm gonna come! I'm coming dammit! I'm coming!

Her beleaguered body bounces against her bonds, shaking the entire fenced area like a third-world earthquake, and a new stream of liquid begins spurting from between her clenched legs, showering Meself in a putrid pool of Joy Juice.

The violent orgasm causes the young woman to pass out and Meself finally allows the peacock feather to float solemnly to the ground, soaking into the stained cement surrounding Joy's barely-breathing broken body. He unlocks and removes the handcuffs, but does not bother taking her down from the showerhead.

Blind-folded Joy later regains consciousness at the touch of a different set of hands, as she feels her body being lowered carefully off the fence. She feels the rough rope being unwound from around her swollen ankles. A cool sponge bath! Someone is giving her a soothingly cool sponge bath. The healing water splashes across her tormented body each time the large sponge makes contact with her skin, whether it is her suffering soles or her soiled snatch. She manages to barely mumble out an expression of gratitude.

Lookie: Thank you…

Snifki: A la orden.

Hearing the Spanish response, Joy swiftly reaches up with her hand and removes her blindfold. Seeing the Mexican respondedor, Joy's brow furrows and her eyes blaze with fury.

Lookie: You! You turned me in for the blankets!

Joy lunges at Jennie, trying to grab for the Latina's throat, but her prone position allows the kneeling Jennie to jump back and avoid Joy's clutches. When Jennie sees her enraged attacker rise to her feet, she throws the soapy sponge at Joy and tries to run in the opposite direction toward the metal tables. Joy runs naked from the shower area, keeping an eye on Jennie, who is seen diving under one of the tables. Joy jumps atop the table and howls, raising her fists in air.

Lookie: SNIFKI!!!

Jennie tries crawling from under the table, but Joy pounces down on top of the girl and the two foes begin rolling across the floor like a lame MMA cage match, naked chick, clothed chick, naked chick, clothed chick… Eventually, Jennie ends up on her back with Joy sitting triumphantly on top of her. Joy pins Jennie's arms to the floor and leans down to press her lips onto Jennie's open mouth.

Snifki: Por favor no!

But Joy sucks Jennie's wagging tongue deep into her mouth and sucks on the lengüeta long and hard, teaching the Latina that the language of love is bilingual. When Jennie quits resisting Joy's advances, Joy breaks off the kiss and sits up straight, swinging her head in circles in a symbolic victory lap, saliva spraying into the air like champagne, while her red hair waves like a finish line flag.

Lookie: SNIFKI!!!

"Cool Hand Job" Scene – Take One

Virginia Foxxx and Star Blaze glare at Joy & Jennie as they enter the basement recreation room, infamously known as the Sugar Shack, walking hand-in-hand to a bench in the corner. Virginia, performing the role of Coffee, approaches the couple with Star (as M'Perry) following closely behind.

Coffee: Yo, newbie. Wha-chu doing with my girl Snifki?

Snifki: I am with Lookie now.

M'Perry: Nobody's talking to you, Snifki! Shut your fur-pie hole!

Coffee: So what makes you so special, fresh fish, that you can come in here and take one o' my girls just like that?

There's a long pause as Joy contemplates (Pause). She puts her arm around Jennie's shoulder and smiles at the Latina, and then she looks Virginia straight in the eyes.

Lookie: I can cram two dozen eggs.

(Pause)

Coffee: Nobody can cram two dozen eggs.

(Pause)

M'Perry: Have you ever crammed two dozen eggs?

Lookie: Nobody's ever crammed two dozen eggs before.

79

Coffee: Then we got a bet here. If you can cram two dozen hard-boiled eggs in your pussy and ass, you can keep Snifki; but if you come up short by even one egg, then the slut comes back to my crew.

Snifki: If my dom says she can cram two dozen eggs, she can cram two dozen eggs!

M'Perry: Yeah, but in how long?

Lookie: A half hour.

M'Perry: Two dozen eggs gotta weigh a good couple pounds. A woman's ass and snatch can't hold that. She'll swell up and bust open. It's gonna kill her.

Coffee: M'Perry, go ask the guard if he can get two dozen hard-boiled eggs from the kitchen.

M'Perry: One rule – no re-cramming. If you let an egg pop out, you forfeit everything.

Snifki: My dom does not re-cram. She will take all twenty-four without losing any.

Virginia and Star walk away from the seated couple, and then Star breaks away in order to locate a guard. Jennie leans over to whisper to Joy.

Snifki: Lookie, why did you have to say two dozen for? Why could you not have said a baker's dozen or twenty?

Lookie: It seemed like a nice round number.

Snifki: Lookie, it is my servitude we are talking about. What is the matter with you?

Lookie: Yeah, well, it gives me something to do.

The audience is now treated to a collage of sequences inside the Sugar Shack, which is basically a white-washed cement block basement area with wide brick pillars and steel beams across the ceiling, along with some border-line obscene murals like one might find in an abandoned subway station. The collage of scenes involves Jennie helping Joy train for the egg challenge, which includes naked squat thrusts and sit-ups, high volume enemas and douches, and double-fisted penetration. Virginia and Star re-enter the Sugar Shack, along with a small portable cooler being carried by Star. Joy is still on her hands and knees, getting fisted by Jennie, whose ambidextrous wrists can be seen alternatingly disappearing inside Joy's ass and pussy, one after the other. Joy has to raise her voice to be heard over the suction and squishing action of Jennie's well-lubed hands.

Lookie: Deeper, harder, stretch me out!

M'Perry: What's with the exercise?

Coffee: Forget it, she's wasting her time.

Meself enters the Sugar Shack area while Jennie pulls her sticky hands out of Joy's posterior. Joy, who is the only naked person in the room, self-consciously twists her body around on the wooden bench until she is seated with her legs dangling over the side. She leans back against the wall, while Jennie busies herself wiping her hands off with a towel.

Guard: Let's get on with this. It's almost time for lights out.

Star drops the cooler in front of Jennie, who leans down to open the lid. Jennie's face expresses surprise at how large a pile twenty-four eggs represents. As she reaches in, she feels one of the smooth eggs and is somewhat relieved to realize that they are already peeled.

Meself takes out a stopwatch.

Guard: Ready. Go!

Jennie positions herself on her knees between Joy and the cooler, and then begins inserting the eggs one at a time inside Joy's vagina.

Coffee: One, two, three...

M'Perry: She's gonna lose a finger, she crams like that!

Coffee: ...four, five...

Joy's face grimaces as Jennie has trouble forcing in the sixth egg.

Lookie: Slow down a little!

Jennie tries to squeeze in the sixth egg, but notices that the other eggs are beginning to poke back out around her fingers. She uses the palm of her hand in a twisting motion to jam the sixth orb inside. Jennie's fingers push the half dozen as deep as possible beyond Joy's strained pussy lips. Joy's face becomes flush and her eyelids clamp shut in pain, like she's preparing to give birth.

M'Perry: Just like a ripe watermelon – wants to bust itself open. Your girl's done for!

Snifki: Quick. Turn around and get on your knees. Come on, Lookie, eighteen more to go.

Jennie starts plopping eggs into Joy's anus. Joy reaches one hand back between her legs to try to hold the first six eggs in her furry basket.

Coffee: ...seven, eight, nine...

Snifki: Going down into the tunnel.

Guard: Fifteen minutes and counting.

Joy is sweating profusely as more and more eggs are slid into her rectum. Jennie makes sure she pushes each egg as deep as possible into Joy's forbidden love canal. Sweat from Joy's hair and neck scatter like raindrops down her bare back and into the gutter of her ass cheeks, providing some extra lubrication to each aborted chicken embryo.

Guard: Ten more minutes.

Coffee: … fourteen, fifteen…

Snifki: Stay loose buddy, just nine more between you and everlasting glory! They are just little old eggs. They are pigeon eggs, that's all – fish eggs, practically.

Joy is now grunting louder and louder after each egg, her closed eyes squeezing out tears and her nose running profusely. She feels like throwing up, but knows that her stomach is not the problem. The strain of the produce packing is causing her face to break out in bright red blotches.

Coffee: … eighteen, nineteen, twenty…

Snifki: Twenty! All right now, get mad at these damned eggs, cram it girl!

Guard: Two minutes to time.

Jennie begins using the twisting palm technique to insert three more eggs, taking the pile down to just one remaining bowel-obstructing ovum.

Lookie: Stuff it in there! Jam it down there! Get it in!

Guard: Five, four, three, two, one, zero…

M'Perry: Hold it! She didn't keep the last one in her pussy!

Snifki: You don't think so, huh? Turn around, Lookie. Well, let's take a look here… That's not an egg; that's her swollen clit! And now I'm going to have me some egg salad!

As soon as Jennie begins eating out Joy, Meself releases his hard cock from the zipper of his trousers and calls Star over to take care of it. She obediently runs over to Meself, drops on her knees and begins stroking his fat dick.

Guard: What we've got here is... failure to ejaculate!

"In Cold Shower" Scene – Take One

After a knife fight where Joy is stabbed with a scrimshaw shank (scene to be filmed later in the shooting schedule), Virginia and Star are found guilty in the attack and are to be punished for their transgressions. Jennie and Star, still dressed in prison clothes, sit together on a cot in one of the cells. Star is busy braiding her long black hair into two separate strands. When the braids are finished, Star reaches under the cot and hands Jennie a book. Star stands up to look outside the bars, the ends of her long braids bouncing off her upper thighs.

M'Perry: James Fenimore Cooper's '*Last of the Mohicans.*' It's yours if you want it.

Snifki: Would you like me to write your mother? I could send her one of your baskets or your moccasins.

M'Perry: Send her my homemade porn DVDs. Maybe now she'll see how desirable I am. The lone wolf. You know, there was a time once when we almost had it made, just the two of us. She was in a fever about some new project up in Steubenville... a brothel for sex tourists. It was gonna make us a fortune – better than a gold mine. But most of all, it was going to be something we never had before – a real home. We got it set up too, just her and me, side by side. The day the last mirror was bolted to the ceiling, she danced right under it. I was never so happy in all my life. It was a beautiful brothel. But no sex tourists ever came. Nobody. We just lived there all alone in that big empty failure – until she couldn't stand the sight of me. I think it happened when I was eating some maize, beans and squash. She started yelling what a greedy selfish bitch I was. Yelling and yelling, until I grabbed her throat. I couldn't help myself. She tore loose and got a fire stick. She said, 'Look at me, girl. Take a good look, 'cause I'm the last living thing you're ever gonna see.' And she pulled the trigger. But the gun wasn't loaded. She began to cry – bawling like a papoose. I went for a long walk. When I got back, the place was dark and the door was locked. All my stuff was piled outside in the snow where she threw it. I walked away and never looked back. I guess the only thing I'm gonna miss in this world is that poor old lady and her hopeless dreams.

Snifki: I'm glad you don't hate your mother anymore.

M'Perry: But I do. I hate her… and I love her.

Meself unlocks the cell door and pulls out a set of handcuffs. Star places her wrists together and extends them toward Meself, who snaps the cuffs on. After closing the cell door, Meself walks Star down an empty corridor containing three floors of cells, which is known as the South Hall. They are on the first floor, but the upper floors are hard to distinguish considering the limited lighting available. They walk halfway down the hall until they reach an old wooden chair, which looks like it could have been used at a guard's desk. A rope with a metal hook on the end hangs ominously over the chair, tied to the second floor railing and swaying softly in the drafty corridor. 89

Without saying a word, Meself unlocks the handcuffs and Star drops her hands to her sides. Star lowers her head and closes her eyes as Meself begins the humiliating task of unbuttoning her shirt. Meself moves behind her and completely removes her shirt, dropping the garment to the floor and leaving Star standing topless. Pulling her arms behind her, he locks the handcuffs on her from behind.

Star still has her eyes closed, but she can sense Meself circling around her again, checking out her bare chest and her two long braids. With the skill of a perverted eagle scout, Meself lifts her left breast with his left hand and grabs the nearby braid with the other. He quickly loops the long braid tightly around her breast twice, securely tucking the end underneath the loop at the top, and instantly taking Star's breath away in a sharp gasp. He performs an identical rigging maneuver on her right breast, creating two balloon-like protrusions jutting forth from her chest. Without wasting any time, Meself recovers the two loose ends of the braids and simultaneously tugs them toward each other near Star's throat. He pulls and tugs at the two opposing braids, tightening the bound breasts and causing Star to cry out. Meself does not stop pulling on the braids until he has enough length on both sides to tie the two ends of the braids together. Her breasts begin to take on the stereotypical red skin associated with her native race.

Meself helps Star step up onto the chair and reaches up to grab the hook swinging in front of her. With some effort, he manages to jam the hook under the knot in her braids. The cold metal against her chest causes Star to begin trembling and shaking. She tries to stand on her tip toes to relieve some of the pressure on her strained breasts. She feels her pants being violently pulled down by Meself. He forces her to step out of her pant legs, even though it is difficult to maintain her balance on the chair. She is now naked on the chair.

Guard: M'Perry, this is a warrant from the Supreme Court of the State of West Virginia. It is by this court order that the execution of this sentence of orgasm by hanging be carried out. Is there anything you want to say, M'Perry?

M'Perry: I think maybe I'd like to apologize, but who to? Who?... Is the Great Spirit in this place too?

Meself kicks the chair away, causing Star's body to bounce in the air and begin dangling at the end of the hook. Her initial scream is followed by loud groans, which echo through the cavernous corridor. Her mind is in a panic, wanting to see a man about a horse or wanting to see a man called horse – she is delirious from the pain, hallucinating like she's in a sweat lodge eating wild mushrooms and peyote, surrounded by brawny braves and mad medicine men, war drums pounding in her head as if her skull is about to explode... someone is violating her with a nightstick. She is no longer in control of her body; her spirit broken, dizzy from the torture, light-headed from the spinning. She feels the rough wooden club penetrating her pussy, but is unable to resist the violent thrusts or the pressure building inside her womb. Her eventual orgasm causes vibrations to travel up the rope and shake the railings on the second floor, causing dust and cement pieces to fall from above like a massive meteor shower. Star has reached her happy hunting ground.

"The Obscene Mile" Scene – Take One

Scene opens with Meself leading a handcuffed Virginia Foxxx down a corridor toward a large room, which is currently used as a museum by the penitentiary. Along the way, they pass Star who is still swinging by her tits. Meself purposely bumps into Star, causing her to begin spinning at the end of the rope. Star is silent, however, not wanting to steal the scene.

Guard: Fly girl, fly girl strutting! Fly girl, fly girl strutting here! Fly girl, we got a fly girl strutting here! Fly girl, we got a fly girl strutting here!

The museum room is the last stop on the regular penitentiary tours and it features an actual electric chair, which was used in the prison since 1952, roped off so that no tourists can attempt any photo-ops with 'Old Sparky.' The room also has a replica of a chain-link holding cell, where doomed prisoners awaited their fate, like the green room of a late night television talk show. Various displays of shanks, drug paraphernalia, inmate art, and prison mementos adorn the walls of the museum.

Meself follows Virginia inside the holding cell and pulls his key ring out.

Guard: Am I gonna have any trouble with you, fly girl?

Virginia silently holds her handcuffed wrists out in front of her.

Guard: Can you talk?

Coffee: Yes, sir, boss. I can talk.

Guard: If I take those cuffs off you, are you gonna be nice?

Virginia nods. Meself removes the handcuffs.

Guard: You can strip.

Coffee: Are you leaving the lights on while I strip? 'Cause I get a little shy with the lights on sometimes… if it's a strange place.

Guard: Hell yes, we're keeping the lights on. We always keep the lights on when you girls get naked.

Meself watches intently as Virginia slowly strips off her prison clothes. She methodically takes off one article of clothing at a time, patiently folding each piece and placing it neatly on the cot. Once she is nude, she instinctively drops to her knees.

Coffee: I'm getting to my knees. I'm prayin', praying lord; lord is my shepherd and so forth and so on. Sorry for all the sick shit I've done and the men I've trampled and everything and I hope they forgive me and I'll never do it again – that's for sure. Still prayin', gettin' right with god.

Guard: Do it quietly, you nasty skank…

Coffee: Sorry, boss.

Guard: Coffee, stand up and step forward.

Meself leads the nude Virginia out of the cell by the arm and walks her toward the wooden electric chair. The felt rope surrounding the platform had already been removed by Meself.

Coffee: Walkin' the mile. Walkin' the mile. Walkin' the obscene mile... Sitting down now. Takin' a seat on Old Sparky… Getting strapped… Getting clamped… Getting wired… Getting electrode.

Virginia has trouble getting her lines out, considering how tightly Meself straps her legs and arms to the heavy wooden chair; places the sharp metal alligator clamps on her nipples and labia; and attaches the cold white adhesive electrode patches on her breasts and inner thighs. Meself also places a black leather hood over Virginia's head and unzips the portion covering her mouth. He gathers the loose wires from the clamps and electrodes, and plugs them into a hand-held PES Dispenser.

Guard: Roll on one!

Meself moves the dials on the device to the One position and Virginia feels a pleasant tingling all across her body.

Guard: Coffee, you've been condemned to orgasm by a jury of your peers – a sentence imposed by a judge of questionable standing in this state. Do you have anything to say before your sentence is carried out?

Coffee: Yeah, I want a fried chicken dinner with gravy on the taters! I want to shit on your chest! I want Lady Gaga to sit on my face, because I'm one horny hoe! Ha, ha, ha!

Guard: Quiet! Shut up!

Coffee: Sorry, boss.

Guard: Coffee, electricity shall now be passed through your body until you come, in accordance with state law. May Nikola Tesla have mercy on your ass... Roll on two!

Meself twists the knobs, one at a time, straight to the Ten position, causing Virginia to attempt to leap from the seat. But the straps hold tight. Her hands clench into fists, her toes curl inward and her head jerks back against the top of the chair.

Coffee: Aiyee!!! I'm frying!!! I'm frying like a tom turkey!!!

Her speech degrades into indecipherable gibberish as spittle seeps from under the hood. Her whole body is quivering and quaking, shivering and shaking, bereaving and baking. Visions of previous unfortunates who occupied the chair surge through her mind. She tries to shake the harrowing thoughts from her head, but the current coursing through her convulsing body only makes their presence more pronounced. Virginia soon loses control over her muscles as the electricity takes over every striation of every fiber of every muscle, circumventing and short-circuiting every nerve and every blood vessel. She fears the orgasm building inside her fractured shell may destroy her and she may become yet another forgotten victim of Old Sparky.

Hot white pain stabs continuously at her breasts and crotch as her bound body arches against the arc of the electricity. She fights desperately to be released from the chair, but knows her only real release will come when her combated clitoris is finally conquered by the charging current. Powerless against the power that be, she shrieks as a behemothic orgasm possesses her body and she is whisked to another plane of consciousness, specifically unconsciousness.

***

After the electrocution scene, Meself announced a break in the shooting. He'd hoped the cast brought along something to munch on, because catering was not part of his final budget.

Following the clean-up of the Sugar Shack scene, Youseff informed Meself that he had found an old passageway to a subbasement, which could serve as an interesting set for a later scene, but Meself didn't want to take a break at that time. Now Meself looked for his brother, so that he could show him the passage.

"Let's not make this break too long," Kay mentioned to Meself. "We've been making good time with the script so far and I don't want to see us fall behind."

"The girls need time to freshen up," Meself responded. "Besides, Youseff wanted to show me something."

Youseff, of course, could always be found wherever the camera was located, keeping a sharp eye on the expensive instrument, since the Canon Pro had been one of the biggest business investments that the brothers had made. Meself also saw that his brother had found something to snack on.

"What the fuck is that?"

"What's it look like?" Youseff answered, sprinkling a little more salt from a cardboard shaker.

"I'm afraid to ask where you got that from."

"You already know where I got it," Youseff chomped.

"That's fuckin' disgusting, Youseff. How can you eat that?"

"I washed it off. Don't worry about it."

"You'd better not get sick before we're done shooting."

"They're great," added Youseff, trying to egg on his brother. "In fact, I've got a couple more if you're hungry. They're still warm."

"Shut the fuck up," Meself concluded. "I thought you wanted to show me some secret room you found."

"Sure, but first I need to lock up the camera in one of the open lockers in the guard room – just in case."

"Okay, but be quick about it, because Kay is keeping an eye on the time."

Behind a large Authorized Personnel Only door in a musty corridor connected to the Sugar Shack, Meself and Youseff entered a large dark space which appeared to be a boiler room, as far as the beams of their flashlights revealed.

"I think this might be the boiler room where that one maintenance guy had his head chopped off," whispered Youseff as if someone was trying to eavesdrop on their conversation.

"Was it a headless ghoul who led you here?"

Ignoring his brother's demeaning question, Youseff pointed his beam to a dusty place in the corner of the room. "But look on the floor here. See that metal ring?"

"Did you already go in there?"

"Hell yes, I went down there. Wait until you see it."

"What if you'd gotten hurt and we couldn't find you?"

"You'd have just kept filming without me, I'm sure."

Watching his brother lift up on the rusty ring and open up a rectangular hole in the floor, Meself agreed, "Yeah, I guess we would have."

Youseff began climbing down some rickety rungs of a rustic ladder and his brother followed close behind. Soon they were inside a cold subterranean chamber with a dirt floor and rotting horizontal wooden planks, nailed to decrepit vertical four-by-four pillars, covering all the walls. One wall displayed sets of heavy iron manacles bolted to a pair of pillars, while the centerpiece of the floor featured an ominous curved wooden bench with leather restraint straps attached.

"This place looks like some kind of medieval dungeon," observed Meself.

"I knew you'd like it."

"But the girls might refuse to even come down here, let alone be restrained in any of these ancient devices."

"I think that bench there is called a Kicking Jenny. I remember reading about it in one of the prison history books. Maybe strap *our* Jennie down to it and see if she kicks?"

"I'm sure I could make her kick..." began Meself, who flashed his flashlight against the plank walls. "Do you think this chamber is even structurally safe? Look at that wall. It looks like it's been patched."

Youseff walked over to the area illuminated by his brother. He leaned down and was able to get some of his fingers in between the odd-looking panels. After a bit of light jiggling, one of the loose planks popped off. Youseff directed his flashlight into the vacancy.

"It looks like some kind of a tunnel."

"You're shittin' me?" Meself responded as he joined his brother, who had already begun pulling at the other loose planks.

Youseff easily pulled off three more planks, including the one closest to the floor. Without waiting for permission, Youseff climbed through the tight hole. Meself watched as his brother disappeared into the dark tunnel.

"Youseff, what the fuck? You don't know what's down there. Get the fuck back here. Do you want to get yourself killed? Youseff… Youseff! Dammit Youseff, where are you?!"

Meself realized that screaming into the dark tunnel was pointless and he felt that he had no choice but to try to follow his brother. "Dammit Youseff, wait up!"

The narrow tunnel had some wooden support beams, but still appeared to be primitive. The ceiling of the tunnel was so low that crawling was the only option of passage. Meself cussed to himself as he found that crawling with a flashlight in his hand was difficult, especially since he was trying to catch up to his brother. He could also imagine Kay upstairs, impatiently pacing the floor and continuously checking her watch and scribbling on her clipboard.

The tunnel seemed endless and Meself was losing steam in his pursuit. He still hadn't caught a sight of his brother and he guessed that he must have crawled about a quarter mile. His sore knees felt like they were on fire. He also had a newfound respect for coalminers and he wished that he had a helmet. The beam of his handheld flashlight did not adequately touch upon the ceiling of the tunnel and he was worried that he would bust his head open on a low-hanging rock.

Meself eventually heard a familiar voice: "Hey, bro!"

"Youseff, stay right there! When I get up there I'm going to kick your ass! My jeans are fucking ruined, I want you to know!"

"Don't worry, I'm not going anywhere."

When Meself reached his brother, he understood why they could go no farther. The tunnel ended against a cement block wall. Youseff was relaxing against the wall, covered in dirt and grime, waiting on Meself's clumsy approach.

"Bro, we shoulda brought a pickaxe."

"A pickaxe? Why, so you can waste a few more hours prospecting?

"Aren't you curious what's behind the wall?"

"Youseff, you could tell me that Miss West Virginia was behind that wall, and that she wants to explore my panhandle, and I still wouldn't care. We have to get back to the set before Kay puts in a call to the Black Hand."

"All right then, I guess we better start crawling back."

"I guess so."

Once again, Youseff took up the lead as the duo began the long journey back toward the prison cellar. Meself wondered whether he'd be able to walk after crawling back through the claustrophobic tunnel.

"Meself..." the brother called from in front.

"What, Youseff?"

"I bet you could fit at least twenty-four people into this orifice..."

"Shut up, Youseff. Please just shut the fuck up."

I sit and lay in my bed,
and hear the words running
through my head.
I think sometimes
I might be dead,
but death can't be this bad.
I sit and lay on my bed,
I can feel the blood
running through my chest.
Sometimes I'll wake in a sweat,
thinking it's blood
running down my chest.
Sometimes I think it's Hell,
but Hell can't be this bad.

- Written on the wall: Floor 2 Block B Cell 14

"People have got to know whether or not their warden is a tyrant. Well, I'm not a tyrant. I've earned everything I've got."

The year was 1973 and West Virginia State Penitentiary Superintendent Colonel Johnny Peck was addressing Assistant Superintendent Captain Willy Wilkinson in the Office of the Warden. Wilkinson, a large muscle-bound middle-aged brute wearing a typical brown guard uniform, sat confidently in a plush leather chair facing Peck's massive desk.

"Of course, sir," Wilkinson replied, glancing around the lavishly decorated office, thinking that the Governor probably didn't have such a nice office.

"Rumors of mistreatment and malnutrition at this fine institution have been heard as far away as central Ohio," complained Peck, who nervously scratched the widening bald spot on his odd-shaped head. "Hell, the Cincinnati Enquirer called me yesterday for comments."

"Sorry to hear that, sir."

"Well, you should be Wilkinson. Anyway, that's why I invited a reporter from the Wheeling Register here today for a tour – a *controlled* tour, if you know what I mean, in order to try to dispel some of these vicious rumors."

"I'm aware of that, sir. We've been preparing all week for the visit."

"Yes, yes, yes."

"The inmates have been cleaning the grounds, the cell blocks and their personal cells. They've also been notified not to speak to any reporter unless we say it's okay. The cafeteria is preparing special meals and the shops all have their best products on display."

"Yes, yes, yes. What about the punishment room? He's going to ask about that, you know."

"Some of the hardware is still there, bolted to the floor and walls, but it looks abandoned, like you wanted."

Peck leaned back in his chair, wiping his brow with a handkerchief. He felt overheated in his three-piece business suit and he was worried about beads of sweat dropping down onto his excessively wide-bottomed pastel neck tie.

"I'm too old for this shit, Wilkinson. But that doesn't mean I want forced into retirement either. I feel like I'm being railroaded, Wilkinson, and I haven't felt like that since I left the South Carolina Railway."

"Sorry to hear that, sir."

"That was a joke, Wilkinson. I was *railroaded* when I was general manager at the *railway*. Get it?"

"Yes, sir, that was quite clever."

Peck studied the emotionless face of his assistant. He'd worked with the physically-intimidating man for over a year, but still really didn't know him. Consequently, he didn't trust Wilkinson. He especially didn't like how Wilkinson was always looking at (or coveting) his fancy glass-doored bookcases, his neatly-framed certificates of appreciation and his well-stocked wet bar.

"Do you always have such a sour disposition, Wilkinson?"

"It comes with the territory, sir."

Peck's secretary interrupted their exchange by cracking open the office door and announcing the arrival of the reporter.

"Send the good fellow in!" Peck responded, standing up from his seat in order to greet the visitor. Without the desk to shield him, Peck's substantial girth was apparent and was indicative of the fact that he certainly did not partake of the prison's regular meals.

Comparatively, the young man who sheepishly entered the office appeared quite skinny and weak in his outdated Nehru jacket – exactly what Peck was hoping to see. He had worried that the newspaper might send one of their world-weary old veterans to cover the story.

"Warden Peck? I'm Reginald from the Register."

"Reggie? Reggie from the Register," greeted Peck, firmly shaking the young man's hand, squeezing his palm with just enough pressure to relay a sense of confidence and persuasion. "Welcome to the West Virginia State Penitentiary."

"Or as some call it: Blood Alley," Reggie from the Register responded.

Peck quickly released the reporter's hand and looked over at Wilkinson, who was just getting up to join his boss. "Blood Alley?" Peck rhetorically reiterated. "I've never heard it called that. Have you ever heard anyone referring to our premier penal institution as Blood Alley, Wilkinson?"

"No sir, I have not."

"Who referred to our prison as Blood Alley, Reginald?... This is my assistant Captain Willie Wilkinson, by the way."

"Oh, I'm sorry, but you know how we reporters are about revealing confidential sources... but it's nice to meet you Captain Wilkinson."

Wilkinson didn't shake the reporter's hand when it was offered, seeing how Peck's handshake failed to leave an impression on the youth. Reginald turned his unaccepted handshake into an awkward salute, and then reached inside his jacket for his small spiral notebook.

"Shall we?"

"Certainly," Peck answered, leading the way to the door. "It's about supper time, so let's head over to the cafeteria. Have you eaten yet, Reginald? Or is that something else you cannot reveal?"

"You might convince me to grab a snack, Warden."

As the three men walked past the secretary's desk, Peck told the stern-looking woman to contact Sister Pearl and tell her that their afternoon bible study will have to be canceled for today.

"Yes, Mr. Peck," the woman sneered.

"Sister Pearl is a volunteer here at the prison, doing the Lord's work," Peck explained to the visitor. "She conducts bible studies and prayer meetings with the inmates, visits the men in the infirmary and conducts a Sunday School class before our regular non-denominational services. I also meet with her toward the end of each day. I find our devotional meetings help reduce the stress that unfortunately goes along with this job, plus our readings help put the day's events in perspective."

"I'm sorry you have to miss today's meeting."

"Not a problem, dear boy. Now, as we make our way down to the cafeteria, allow me to tell you a little bit about the facility. The prison began as a wooden structure on this site in 1866 with just seven inmates and one warden. A little over a hundred years later, these stone walls now span over five acres and we have about eighteen hundred inmates."

"Would you say there's a problem with overcrowding?"

"Not particularly. Do you think there's a problem with overcrowding, Wilkinson?"

"Not particularly, sir."

"I tend to think the more the merrier," Peck added. "Two or three inmates to a cell, I think, promotes a sense of camaraderie or family, you know, brotherly love and all that."

"I see."

"Of course you do, dear boy, of course you do. Now, the West Virginia State Penitentiary is the state's largest and most important penal institute. It is almost a hundred percent self sufficient, having a number of workshops inside the walls, plus a working farm and a coal mine a few miles off site. You'll be enjoying some of the fruits of the prisoners' labor very shortly."

"I assume you mean from the farm and not the coal mine, Warden."

"Precisely, Reginald, you're a very clever lad, very clever indeed. Don't you agree, Wilkinson?"

"Yes, sir, that was quite clever."

As they walked down the main hall leading to the cafeteria, Reginald glanced out one of the windows which faced into the prison yard. He stopped for a moment to get a closer look.

"Do my eyes deceive me or are those men actually playing badminton and croquet?"

"Oh yes," answered Peck, looking back to give Wilkinson a surreptitious smile. "Our men enjoy the more refined recreational activities, especially now that Spring has sprung. You'll see no sweaty tattooed body-building or nasty shirts-versus-skins basketball games in our yard."

"Ah yes, Springtime," commented Reginald, still eyeing the awkward croquet players, "when a young man's fancy lightly turns to thoughts of rover hoops and scatter shots."

"There you go with that sharp wit of yours again, Reginald. That was a good one."

Reginald watched as one of the inmates in the croquet game finally realized he was being watched from inside the hall. The inmate raised his mallet and shook it at the spectators, following up with a resounding, "FUCK YOU!"

"What's the man with the mallet yelling?" Reginald asked. "I can't hear him from inside here."

"I believe he's yelling, 'Tally-Ho'," Peck answered.

"Tally-Ho?"

"Yes, yes, yes, it's some kind of friendly greeting that is traditionally associated with the noble game of croquet. Come now, we must make haste to the cafeteria before our reservations expire."

"Reservation?"

As Peck and the journalist restarted their journey, Wilkinson lagged behind a bit to return the inmate's so-called greeting, waving his billy club at the man outside. The man quickly lowered his mallet and looked silently to the ground.

When they reached the velvet-draped doors of the cafeteria, the trio was immediately welcomed by an elderly maître d'prison, who was hunched over in an ill-fitting tuxedo and displayed a white cloth wrapped over his left forearm. "Table for three today, gentleman? I believe I remember the reservation."

"Yes, sir," Peck responded.

"Please follow me. Your table is ready."

The men walked into the dimly lit dining room, past rows of quiet inmates seated at long tablecloth-adorned tables. Each table had three decorative centerpieces, including flickering candles in stained-glass holders and freshly-cut flowers in colorful Fenton vases. In the far corner of the room, a violinist and a pianist were playing selections of light classical music.

As the men took their seats at one of the few circular tables, which were reserved for the guards, Reginald commented, "This is definitely not what I expected."

"Well, what did you expect my dear boy? Did you think we tossed stale bread and rancid water through the bars of the cells?"

Reginald turned over the heavy pastel-colored plate in front of him and confirmed his suspicion of the Fiestaware stamp. "No, I just wasn't expecting all this."

"The inmates find that classical music and the overall ambience of fine dining helps with digestion. Isn't that right, Wilkinson?"

"I haven't had the desire to belch in months, sir."

The maître d'prison waited until the gentlemen finished their initial conversation before recommending the herb-crusted roast beef tenderloin with parmesan cheese. All three ordered the special, specifying various levels of preparation from medium rare to well done, and named their personal choices of salad dressing and potato-based (pronounced pōe-tăt-tōe) side item.

Taking a sip from his crystal ice water glass, Reginald added, "In fact, the only thing that doesn't surprise me is the plastic silverware."

"A safety precaution, of course, but thankfully the meat is always so tender that the plastic utensils are never a problem."

When the meals were promptly delivered to their table, the Colonel's words proved true as everything on the plate could be easily carved, sliced and skewered with the plastic forks and knives, just like cutting through butter, and that included the hand-churned butter provided for the fresh rolls.

The men avoided talking prison business during their meal, preferring to chat about less important subjects, such as the Watergate investigation and the reduction of troops in Vietnam. But during the dessert course of Chocolate-Nut Torte, Reginald could not resist bringing up the unsavory subject of cruel and unusual punishment.

The question came while Peck was pushing his fork down into his cake, causing the first plastic prong to touch the plate to break off and fly across the table. Peck looked at his broken fork and pushed the plate toward the center of the table in disdain.

"Well, I had hoped to show you our prison industries after supper, but if that unsettling subject is first and foremost on your mind, I suppose it's best to get it out of the way. Since I have never been there personally, I will have Captain Wilkinson lead us down to the basement area where corporal punishments once took place. Please remember that methods of punishment in prisons have caused a great deal of debate in almost every state and these methods have been changed many times over the years. Some remnants of previous methods practiced behind these walls are still present, mainly to serve as reminders of how far we've progressed as an institution. As the superintendent of this prison, my belief is that good food, clean clothing, healthy surroundings, religious instruction, and a library full of the finest literature and inspirational material, are of more benefit in securing good behavior than all the cruel inhuman punishments that can be inflicted. But do you know what is most troubling to me, Reginald?"

"What would that be, sir?"

"That you didn't write down any of what I just said."

Not waiting for any further response from the journalist, Peck and Wilkinson stood up from the table and Reginald soon followed. Wilkinson led the way down to the basement, through the Sugar Shack, into the boiler room and down the hatch in the floor.

A single light bulb hung from an extension cord in the center of the crudely constructed subbasement room, shining its glare on the wood plank walls, the dirt floor and a few assorted restraint devices.

The centerpiece of the room was, of course, a strange wooden bench on a cement slab. The bottom of the wooden bench was bolted into the cement and then curved upward into a quarter-circle. It was obvious that a prisoner would be forced to lie over the curved bench on his stomach and then have his hands and feet manacled to the floor. The manacles were still present, along with some leather straps.

Reginald shivered, either from the cool temperature or the horrid décor, noting, "This place is downright medieval. What the hell is that bench contraption?"

"It's called a Kicking Jenny," Wilkinson explained. "Go ahead and lie across it if you want."

"I don't know about that. I'm no George Plimpton, if you know what I mean."

"Don't worry about it, Reginald; Captain Wilkinson is not going to lock you down. Right, Wilkinson, you weren't going to lock him in?"

"No, we don't *have* to lock him in, sir," admitted Wilkinson.

"But you were, right?" Reginald's inquiring mind wanted to know. "You had every intention of locking me down on that, that thing."

"It's called a Kicking Jenny," Wilkinson reminded him. "And no, I wasn't going to lock you down on it."

"Okay," mumbled Reginald, slowly approaching the curved bench, "but it sure as hell sounded like you were going to…"

Reginald hesitantly leaned over the curved bench, his glam-looking boots standing between two iron manacles at the foot of the bench, where the wood met the cement, while his head and neck protruded just over the top edge. He noticed that his arms, which dangled over each side, could be easily pulled down and secured in the second set of manacles. To a witness, it would look like he was leaning over an invisible barrel.

"Usually the disobedient inmate would be naked," Wilkinson explained, almost with glee. "But once he is secured to the Kicking Jenny, a guard would bring out a heavy leather strap, consisting of two three-foot long strips of sole leather, and would viciously beat the prisoner until he was unconscious."

Reginald jumped off the bench like it was on fire.

Changing the subject, Reginald pointed to some manacles hanging high off a beam along one wall, "What were those used for?"

"Those?" answered Wilkinson. "Those manacles were used to secure a prisoner in the standing position for a punishment called The Shoo-Fly. The inmate's arms were secured above his head, and his feet were also manacled to the floor. A device was then used to keep the prisoner's head locked in one position. Once secured, a fire hose was pulled down from the boiler room and water would be sprayed into the prisoner's face until he would be close to drowning."

Silence engulfed the room as the men pictured the water torture in their minds. But then some scratching sounds were heard, along with a muffled voice saying something like, "What the fuck?"

The three men looked at one another to ascertain who may have blurted out the obscenity. They then heard more pronounced scratching, as if large rodents were being disturbed behind one of the plank-covered walls. Or perhaps it was the spirits of the dead, the restless souls who had died in agony in this very room?

"This is freaking me out," whispered Reginald. "I think I've seen enough down here."

Their mutual attention focused on one wall in particular, where the scratching seemed to be emanating. Suddenly a booted foot crashed through the wall, sending a splintered plank thumping to the dirt floor.

"Holy shit!" screamed Reginald, running blindly to the opposite side of the room, like something was breaking through the wall to come get him.

"What the hell is that, Wilkinson?" demanded Peck.

Wilkinson stomped over to the flailing foot in the wall and grabbed it with both hands. He could hear someone on the opposite side of the wall commanding him to let go, but Wilkinson responded with one herculean pull, which sent a man's entire body smashing through several planks and dropping violently to the floor. Wilkinson proceeded to beat the frightened man into submission with his baton, sending crushing blows to the man's skull until there was no further movement from the intruder.

But then another man popped his head out of the hole in the wall, asking, "What do you guys think you're doing?"

Wilkinson grabbed the second man by the hair and dragged him head first out of the wall, and then began beating him into unconsciousness. The sickening sound of the wooden club crushing into a boney skull made Reginald crumple to the floor and cover his ears.

"My god!" exclaimed Reginald. "What's happening here?! I want to leave this instant!"

***

Drifting through the tumultuous stream of pain, stream of light, stream of consciousness... Head floating, rolling, dipping in and out of the waves... Breathing, gasping, choking... Daydreams, night dreams, day terrors, night terrors... Sleep patterns, ceiling tile patterns, flight patterns... Trances, visions, still pictures, scenes... An angel, a nurse, a woman... Praying, talking, asking... Memories, mammories, melodies... Dogs, spotted, watched... Barking, running, pulling... Circling, surrounding, surfing... Man, men, people... Brother...Brother...

"Brother..."

Night...

Youseff tried to raise his swollen head and look over to the bed beside him, but his neck felt like a steel pipe and stinging pain shot into his brain. He knew his brother was lying next to him in another bed, because he could hear Meself's familiar snoring. They were in a hospital? They were in a hospital with angels and dogs? All dogs go to heaven? Youseff drifted back to sleep.

"Brother..."

Day...

Meself tried to sit up in his bed, but only managed to turn over on his side. The new position allowed him to see his brother and to avoid the bright rays of early morning sunlight shining through the windows. His puffy eyebrows made it hard to squint. Another day… another concussion.

"Youseff, you fucktard, wake up."

Youseff stirred a bit, but didn't respond.

Meself raised his voice an octave, calling again, "Youseff, *wake up.*"

"Mmmama," Youseff mumbled. "Mama, Meself is being mean again. Make him stop."

"Youseff, snap out of it. *Wake up, man.*"

"I don't want to go to school."

"*Youseff…*"

Meself heard the familiar click of heels on tile and soon an attractive woman in a white dress came into his field of vision. The blonde instantly reminded him of photographs he'd seen of Marilyn Monroe – not the glamour shots, but the autopsy photos where her hair is slicked back and she has a vacant look on her face.

"Hush now, you're disturbing the other men in the ward," she leaned down and whispered. "You need to let your friend sleep too. Would you like me to get you some breakfast?"

"Yes, please."

"You'll have to turn back over on your back then, so I can position the tray."

The woman helped him roll back over, but Meself found it unusual that she had one of her hands directly over the place on the blanket where his crotch was located.

"Take it easy on the bladder there, nursey."

"I'm *not* a nurse."

Meself heard squeaky wheels approaching and strained to look past the non-nurse, who quickly squeezed his morning erection through the blanket before letting go. "I'll grab you a bedpan also," she whispered.

He was going to comment about her obvious effort to cop a feel, but realized that the wheels he heard were attached to a small four-wheeled creeper. He was stunned to see what appeared to be a legless man sitting on the creeper – and was even more surprised to see two greyhound dogs pulling the cart like a miniature sleigh. The man on the creeper glared straight at Meself as he drove by the bed. The dogs also growled.

"What in the hell is that?" asked Meself.

"Oh, pay him no mind," she said. "Let me go fetch your things."

"Meself," weakly called Youseff from the neighboring bed. "Meself, what's going on? Why are there dogs pulling people around?"

The woman turned her attention to Youseff. "You need to hush too. You're not the only men on this floor. I suppose you'd like breakfast and a bedpan too?"

"Yes, ma'am."

As the woman's heels clicked away, both brothers struggled until they were sitting up in their beds. They looked up and down the large dormitory-style room, trying to get another look at the strange man on the dog-drawn creeper. But all they could see were more beds like the ones they were on, containing more men like the ones they considered themselves to be.

"Where are we, Meself? I don't like it here."

"I don't know, it looks like some kind of hospital, but I don't think veterans' hospitals even look as dreadful as this."

"Why did that guard beat us, Meself? I thought we had the prison reserved."

"We did, Youseff, maybe we interrupted something we weren't supposed to see. Maybe that's why the tunnel was boarded up when we crawled back through. I know as much as you do and that ain't much."

"This sucks."

"Tell me about it."

The woman soon returned pushing a cart. "I've got y'all's bedpans and breakfast."

"Isn't that a Disney movie?" asked Youseff.

"I'm glad to see you're keeping in good spirits," the woman said as she positioned the pans and trays in the appropriate configuration. She seemed to have a bit of difficulty with Meself's bedpan, commenting that she may need to find a larger size for him.

"What is this supposed to be?" Meself asked.

"It's a bedpan, silly, you're supposed to pee in it."

"No, I mean the food. What kind of breakfast is this? It looks more like gruel."

"Just because you're in the infirmary, doesn't mean you get special food," she answered.

"What are you talking about?"

Youseff had already started digging into his pseudo-porridge. "I kind of like it," he interrupted.

The woman immediately turned to Youseff and chastised him. "Excuse me, sir, I know you are hungry, but we must say Grace before we partake in our food."

Youseff sheepishly put his plastic spoon back on his tray and both men remained quiet as the woman said an especially long prayer, thanking God for the men's recovery, for the fine medical care they were receiving, for the shelter they were being provided, and, finally, for the nutritious food they were about to eat. As the prayer was being prayed, both men opened their prayer-respecting eyes when they heard the dogs and the creeper man wheeling slowly past, still glaring and growling at the brothers in a most angry fashion.

Before the woman left them again, Meself repeated his question about the infirmary.

"It's the prison infirmary, of course," she explained as she was leaving. "Where did you think you were, silly?"

Meself looked over to Youseff, who was already eating his gruel. Meself rolled his eyes as he watched his brother shovel spoonful after spoonful of the questionable concoction into his mouth, only stopping periodically to gulp down some room temperature milk.

"Youseff."

Youseff ignored him, concentrating on his food.

"*Youseff.*"

Youseff put down his spoon and glanced with one eye over to his brother as he drank some more milk out of his half empty glass. After licking some milk residue from his upper lip, he answered his brother, "Yeah, what's up?"

"What's up? What's up?! Did you not hear what that chick said?"

"She's glad that I am keeping in good spirits."

115

"Not that, you dipshit. She said we were in a *prison* infirmary."

"So you think she was joking or what?"

"No, I don't think she was joking. Look at this place. It *looks* like a prison infirmary."

"It can't be," Youseff surmised as he picked up his spoon again. "That wouldn't make sense."

"Would you put the fucking spoon down, Youseff? This is serious. We have to figure out what the fuck is going on."

Youseff tossed his spoon onto the tray, realizing that his breakfast would soon get cold if he didn't help Meself assess their situation.

"Okay," Youseff assessed. "Maybe we're both in comas and imaging this whole setting."

"Comas? We're both in a coma?"

"Yes, and we're imaging all this in a sort of dream-like state."

"Youseff, sometimes I think you've been living in a dream-like state since the day you were born."

"There you go. You ask me for my opinion and then you insult me. I'm going to eat my breakfast now."

"I didn't think your educated opinion was going to involve some existential mumbo jumbo about being in a dream-like state."

"Well, it does; and it makes perfect sense if you think about it."

"No it doesn't make sense. Not a lick of sense."

"Why not?"

"Okay, are you surmising that we are both in a coma and dreaming the exact same thing simultaneously?"

"Well, we are twins."

"Being twins has nothing to do with it. How could we both be dreaming about this very conversation?"

"Maybe only one of us is in a coma and dreaming, while the other one is lucid and patiently holding a bedside vigil."

"What?"

"You heard me. I'm aware of this conversation taking place, so it's perfectly feasible that this is *my* imagination and I am just dreaming this whole conversation."

"Then you must like calling yourself an idiot, because that's what I'm adding to the conversation."

"Whatever, Meself... I think, therefore I am."

"Well, it just so happens that I'm the one who is cognizant of this conversation, so maybe you're the one holding the bedside vigil for me."

"How can that be, when you won't accept the original theory that one of us is in a coma? I mean you can't argue in favor of the conclusion if you don't support the hypothesis."

"Hypothesis? You must be the one high on pot. Listen, if I pinch myself, I can feel it, but you can't, so that satisfies my state of perception."

"But I have to *believe* that you can feel yourself getting pinched, because I can pinch myself just as easily and come to the same conclusion."

"Okay, okay then, you don't have to believe me that I can feel myself getting pinched. But let's try this: I will think of a number between one and ten. If this is wholly your dream and not mine, then you should be able to guess my number correctly if you so desire."

"All right, I'll say your number is three."

A disgusted look came over Meself's face and he looked helplessly to the ceiling.

"Three?" Meself confirmed. "Dammit, I was thinking of three. Forget that test."

"Let me ask you this, Meself. Knowing your own process of problem solving or your personal style of rationalization, can you state emphatically that you would *ever* have come up with my theory that at least one of us is in a coma and dreaming this whole scenario?"

"Of course not. I would never propose something so ridiculous."

"Then that proves this cannot possibly be *your* dream."

"What? Now my head is really starting to pound."

"Never mind, Meself. Why don't you just come up with a better explanation than my coma theory to explain our bizarre predicament?"

While Meself was contemplating a response, he saw the man with no legs coming down the center of the hall on his dogsled. "Maybe we were both killed and this is some kind of purgatory," Meself offered.

The man on the cart pulled back on the reins as he approached the beds of the brothers. The dogs growled in response to the sudden command, their pointy heads getting tugged painfully backward.

"Did I hear somebody say they thought they were in purgatory?" asked the man, whose head bobbed just above the visual plane of the mattresses. "You're actually closer to hell."

When more of the wiry man's torso became visible at the foot of the bed, Meself realized that the man was apparently pulling himself up by climbing the blanket, which hung off the edge of the bed. At one point it looked like the man might be losing his grip and was in danger of falling to the floor.

"Gimme a fuckin' hand will ya?" he begged Meself. "Can't you see I'm struggling here?"

Meself pushed his tray out of the way and leaned down toward the mattress climber, even though the effort accentuated the continuing pain inside his battered back and head. Meself grabbed the man's wrist and pulled him onto the top of the bed. Meself wondered whether the man's legless body would leave stains on his bed like some kind of a mutant snail.

The thin man appeared to be in his forties and had a buzz cut hair style similar to the other residents in the infirmary. His facial features were hard and jagged, like his head was sculpted from the same sandstone that was used to construct the penitentiary, and his eyes were dark and beady. He wore a typical tan prison shirt, but it was long enough to hide his disjoined joints.

"Welcome to Blood Alley," he announced once he got his balance on the soft mattress. "I'm Paul Hankish. Or should I say welcome *back*?"

"Welcome?" blurted Meself. "You haven't exactly made us feel real welcome, cruising back and forth with your scowling face and growling dogs."

"Well, I have every right to be upset with you two, since you've probably ruined my escape plans. The screw says you two were hiding in the tunnel beneath the boiler room..."

"Wait a second," Youseff chimed in. "What do mean by Blood Alley? Where the hell are we anyway?"

"What? Are you two nuts? You're in the infirmary at the West Virginia State Penitentiary."

Meself responded, "Don't call *us* nuts. You're the one trying to escape from a jail that's been closed for like twenty years."

"Listen boys, I don't know what all damage that billy club has done to y'all's head bones, but this pen has been up and running continuously for a hundred years."

"That's just not true," Meself contended. "We had the facility booked for a movie shoot. We were supposed to have the run of the place until dawn. Getting clubbed by some maniac, who wasn't even supposed to be on the property, was not part the contract."

"You're seriously confused and unless you want locked up in the dark cell for being nuts, I'd strongly recommend you not tell the guards or the warden that you think the prison is closed down for you to make a movie."

Youseff added, "My brother is right though. Our company is called JB Video Arcade and we are making a movie inside the West Virginia Penitentiary. During a break in the production, I showed my brother a tunnel I found while exploring an area beneath the boiler room. We tried to crawl through the tunnel, but the far end was cut off with cement blocks."

"Yeah," agreed Meself, "so we tried crawling back the way we came and then discovered our point of entry had been boarded up."

Paul listened intently to the story and studied the brother at the head of the bed. The silence between the three men became uncomfortable as various strange scenarios raced through all their minds. The dogs picked up on the tension and began to whine.

Paul finally rubbed his chin and guessed, "You two know it's nineteen seventy-three, don't you?"

"What d'ya mean?"

"I mean the year is nineteen seventy-three, you know that, right?"

Meself listened intently to the question and studied the amputee at the foot of the bed. The silence between the two and a half men became uncomfortable as various strange scenarios raced through all their minds. The dogs picked up on the added tension and began to growl.

Meself glanced over at his brother and nodded, and then looked Paul in the eyes. "Buddy, you *are* fuckin' insane. We *must* be in some kind of mental ward. I've got to get up out of this bed and get the fuck out of here... like now."

Paul laughed, "You guys aren't going anywhere... and keep your voices down."

"I'm not kidding," concluded Meself, straining to swing his legs off the edge of the bed and almost knocking Paul off balance. "Youseff, you've got to try to get up too. We're going to sign ourselves out of this place or find someone to let us leave."

"Good luck on that," Paul responded, still laughing at the boys' predicament. "If you want to know why you're here, I might be able to explain it."

One of the greyhounds tried to snap at Meself's exposed feet, so he pulled his legs back under the blanket. "Okay, explain away, mister, but try to make some sense this time."

"You're familiar with the Grave Creek Mound across the street?"

"Yeah," answered Youseff. "It's part of the Delf Norona Museum. We used to go there all the time on school field trips."

"It's become a museum, eh? That's interesting."

"There's a gift shop and everything. It's run by the state."

"Well, it's actually a very sacred place. It wasn't just a burial mound for the Adena Indians. It was also a mystical place where they held ceremonies to conjure the spirits of the dead; supposedly bringing the dead back to life."

"Here we go again..." said Meself, rolling his eyes.

"No, hear me out. The tunnel you were in goes directly under the mound. I know it does, because I supervised its construction. It was supposed to exit into a burial chamber where the first Adena chief was laid to rest – not burned like the others. But we never broke through to the chamber. I wonder if the new museum found the chamber and sealed it up with cement."

Youseff perked up. "I get it! When the tunnel breached the mound, it could've become some kind of wormhole or time warp, mimicking the way the Adena used the mound to bring back the dead."

"Okay," interrupted Meself, "but I only have one question."

"What's that?" asked Paul.

"Why aren't you cuddled up on my brother's bed, since you both seem to share the same mental illness?"

"You can mock all you like," warned Paul. "But I've studied this phenomenon both inside and outside the pen. The key element needed for a traversable wormhole is negative energy and I'd say you brought plenty of it into the tunnel with you."

"Whatever."

"I've also practiced necromancy and have learned many of the ancient secrets of the Adena."

"Spare me."

Paul asked, "You ever hear of the Serpents Club?"

"Nope," answered Meself.

"Yes, you have," corrected Youseff. "We was just there."

"Well, I founded the Serpents Club and ran my operations out of there until that bastard Bill Lias rigged my car with the bomb that blew my legs off. The club was also where me and some others practiced the black arts. If you want to control this territory, you gotta practice the craft. This whole area is saturated with evil spirits, going back thousands of years. Why do think the Micks located the diocese for the whole state in Wheeling?"

"This would make a good regional movie," volunteered Youseff, who was all 'eers.

"Don't encourage him, Youseff," Meself chimed in.

Paul ignored Meself's skepticism, asking instead, "By the way, who was runnin' the club when you was there?"

"Don't go there, Youseff," Meself interceded.

Youseff answered, "Some old dude, calls himself the Black Hand."

"*Dammit*, Youseff!"

"The Black Hand, you say? I'm not sure who that would be, but I'm hoping it's not that back-stabber Melvin Pike from Uniontown. I heard they was grooming that kid to take over Wheeling."

"This guy didn't seem like a *Melvin* to me."

"Maybe it's Bill Lias," sarcastically suggested Meself.

"As a matter of fact, fat ass Lias died three years ago," Paul said matter-of-factly, looking down at his open palm. "But this Black Hand intrigues me. I wonder if he calls himself that because he represents the *five* families."

The men heard someone purposely clear her throat, and then heard the familiar click of heals on linoleum. The mystery woman was approaching from the far end of the infirmary.

"Hey, listen and listen quick," Paul blurted out in a hushed tone. "Remember what I said about not telling the screws *anything* about where you came from – or you'll end up in solitary for the rest of your life. Plus stay away from that crazy bitch coming up the hall.

Warden Pecker has been screwin' her and he don't like anyone else touching her."

"Point taken," Meself replied.

"Tsk-tsk-tsk, Mr. Hankish," chastised the approaching woman. "You need to let these men rest."

"Sorry, Pearl."

She delicately stepped over the dogs and the cart, which had moved between the brothers' beds, and leaned over to grab Hankish around the midsection. She picked the man up, grunting a bit for dramatic effect, and plopped the paraplegic onto his portable platform.

The middle of the night seemed an odd time for a sponge bath, but who was Meself to question the timing? Pearl carefully nudged Meself awake and showed him a large sponge as soon as he opened his eyes.

"I stayed late because I thought you'd like a bath this evening."

Meself glanced around the dark hall, where only scattered ceiling lights were on. He couldn't really discern any of the other men, but could hear many of them snoring.

"Sure," he whispered. "By the way, did you know that I'm a movie director on the outside? I've told my partner over there that you have the looks of a movie star. As soon as we get out of this place, I'd like to get you into some of our films."

"Sounds heavenly," she replied as she pulled down Meself's coverings, leaving him exposed in a thin hospital-type gown.

Pearl pulled up the gown, revealing Meself's naked body, and he helped pull the garment up over his head. She positioned her cart, which had a small water basin on the top, close to the side of the bed.

Meself was pleasantly surprised to see the woman step back and begin unbuttoning her white uniform, starting at the top and working her way down. Her full naked breasts, bearing fresh roseola buds, were the first fruit to sprout forth from her blooming blouse. Soon the unfolding of her widening skirt proved to be the next fertile patch to bear fruit, the fragrant scent filling Meself's nostrils with the promise of Spring.

Perhaps eternal, Spring had indeed sprung from his own private orchard, the arc hardening to reveal a perennial pink petal at its pinnacle. Pearl pounced upon the polarly prostrated prisoner, straddling the naked man with her bent legs wrapped around his shoulders and her low-hanging fruit dangling just above his face. She grabbed her wet sponge from the cart and began watering his growth, while he resigned himself to the water sport known as Pearl diving.

Cognizant of the comatose company contained within the confines of the clinic, both bed-partners did their best to mute their mutual moaning and murmuring. Meself's modulations were *muff*led as he concentrated on the job in front of him, not even noticing when the cool dampness from Pearl's sponge transferred seamlessly to the warm dampness of Pearl's mouth.

Pearl's clam-like mouth clamped onto Meself's mantle and began covering the irritated organ with her saliva, hardening the shiny shaft to pulsating perfection. She took his cock deep to the very depths of her being, breathing in the musty scent of his ball sack.

Without audible signals to guide him toward the goal, Meself relied on the contractual vibrations picked up by his tenacious tongue to tell him when he was close to scoring. But soon Pearl's defenses decided to take a time out and she pulled away from the playing field, turned her body around and converted her sixty-nine formation into a seated-on nine formation. Pearl rode that nine-inch line for all she was worth, giving her head coach one hundred percent.

It was the bedsprings which were now being sprung internal, squeaking and thumping with abandon. Pearl bit down hard on her lip, desperately trying not to scream out while Meself tightened his grip on her wavering waist. Like trying to hold down a rocket, which had already been ignited, Meself eventually had to release his cache of jet fuel as Pearl sprung down hard on top of his chest.

The two clung to each other, sweaty and breathing hard, exhaustively listening for anything or anyone to stir within the dark room. How could no one have heard their frantic finale? Then, like crickets chirping randomly in the night, the subtle sounds of bedsprings, which usually accompany the act of sequestered self-satisfaction, arose within the room.

Captain Wilkinson spread out a collection of confiscated items on Peck's previously empty, smooth-n-shiny desktop. As Peck began to pick through the paraphernalia, Wilkinson took his usual seat opposite the desk. Peck paid particular attention to a black cell phone, which he tried shaking like a rattle.

"What the hell is this, Wilkinson?"

127

"I don't know. Looks like a phone to me."

"A phone? How can it be a phone? Do you see a cord, Wilkinson?"

"No, sir, I don't see a cord."

"Then it can't very well be a telephone, can it?"

"I guess not, sir. Good observation, sir."

Peck found a gap in the plastic at the bottom of the device and pried the lid open with his fingernail, revealing a numbered keypad and a small screen. "This looks like some kind of phone, Wilkinson."

"That's what I thought, sir."

"Did you ask those dumb asses in the infirmary what it is?"

"Yes, sir, but they claimed they didn't know. In fact, they're both claiming amnesia, complaining that the assault caused them to forget everything, including who they are and what they were doing in the tunnel."

"Hmm, but we know who they are, correct, Wilkinson?"

"Well, their faces are pretty beat up and swollen, but we believe they're the Rodriguez brothers, who we thought escaped last week from the Fairchance farm. They were trustees, unfortunately."

"But trusted no more, Wilkinson. Trusted no more."

"Yes, sir. They'll be placed back in the general population as soon as they're released from the infirmary."

"So, do you think they were down in that tunnel since last week?"

"Very likely, sir. The troubling thing is that someone inside must have supplied them with sustenance, civilian clothing and these other items."

"Yes, these IDs and credit cards in the wallets look nice, but there's something odd about them. I can't quite put my finger on it…"

"The cards and identification are all forgeries. Whoever manufactured them on the outside must have been playing a joke on the prisoners, because all that stuff is dated over forty years into the future. I doubt those men downstairs would have had much luck on the outside with those cards."

"Hell, Wilkinson, and look at these small brass coins. They're supposed to be one dollar coins, but I don't see any dates on them… and these presidents have never been on any coins I've ever seen. Isn't Ike supposed to be on the silver dollar?"

"Obvious counterfeits, sir. Try spending them at a newsstand and I bet the Feds will be onto you in no time."

"This is all so strange, Wilkinson," Peck added, picking up the cell phone again after sliding the coins into his top desk drawer. "I'm wondering if these men are the ones who have been reporting our business to the press – maybe using this device as some kind of radio transmitter."

"That's possible, sir. It may have been manufactured to ensure that no one else can use it, except for the person it was made for, like some kind of spy tool."

"You know what I think, Wilkinson?"

"What do you think, sir?"

"I think we need to closely observe these men, Wilkinson. I'd love to know exactly what they are up to and I sure as hell want to know who's been helping them... Let's make like there will be no repercussions for their escape attempt, except for being moved to the general population. Put them together in a cell and monitor it closely."

"Do you want me to seal up the tunnel?"

"Actually, no, Wilkinson, let's leave it as is for the time being. Maybe it'll serve as an incentive for them to continue with their plans. Lock the hatch door in the boiler room though. Let's not make it too easy for them."

"Yes, sir."

"Make sure you keep checking with all your informants too. Make them understand this investigation is a priority."

"I'm glad you brought that up, sir," replied Wilkinson, pausing for effect. "Do I have permission to speak freely?"

"Of course you do, Wilkinson, this isn't the damn Marine Corps."

"I understand that, sir. It's just that one of the rats in the infirmary told me Pearl seems to have taken a liking to one of the brothers and has been spending a lot of time near his bed."

"Is that right? Pearl, you say? Well, once this investigation is over and done with, I want you to make sure both of these brothers are also over and done with. Do you understand me, Wilkinson?"

"It would be my pleasure, sir," he concluded, stroking away at the baton at his side as he smiled knowingly at Peck.

***

"Wakey, wakey, egg and pancakey!"

Wilkinson tossed a set of gray prison garb at the foot of each bed and began banging the metal bed frames with his baton. Both startled brothers awoke at the racket as the rhythm of the baton strikes reminded them of the day the baton banged into their skulls.

"Wha-what?!" sputtered Youseff.

"I've got good news for you cons," Wilkinson announced with a grin. "The doc says you're cleared to go to general pop."

"General Pop?" asked Youseff. "Who's that?"

"General population, moron," Wilkinson answered. "So get your asses out of bed and get dressed."

"Wait, wait a second," Meself protested. "What doctor cleared us? There's been no doctor coming around to check on us."

Wilkinson waved the club toward Meself. "I've got the release form right here. Do you wanna take a closer look?"

"Point taken," Meself concluded as he reached down to gather his uniform.

As the brothers dressed, Meself asked if there was a way to get a message to Pearl, perhaps through Paul. Wilkinson had a hearty laugh over the request.

"No Legs ain't your personal message boy," he responded. "Besides, Pearl is the last person in this institution that you should be communicating with."

The brothers slipped on their ill-fitting prison-issue shoes while Wilkinson impatiently tapped the baton against his palm. As soon as the siblings were standing, Wilkinson pointed the baton in the direction that he wanted the men to precede.

From the infirmary to the Main Corridor, Meself and Youseff marched single file with Wilkinson following close behind. As they approached the South Hall, the brothers could hear the disturbing din of the cell block getting louder and louder, while their mutual feeling of dread became more and more pronounced.

By the time Wilkinson deposited the men in the first cell on the corner upon entering the block, both men were visibly shaken. Wilkinson chuckled as the cell door slammed shut, observing, "You cons act like you never been locked up before."

The other inmates were yelling and taunting the new arrivals from the cells above and beside the brothers, but neither Meself nor Youseff responded to the guard's observation. As soon as Wilkinson walked away, the brothers inspected their shallow five-by-seven foot cell. A double metal bed rack was suspended from the wall, containing two thin mattresses with matching thin blankets. A toilet and a metal sink took up most of the remaining space.

Youseff sat down on the lower bed, assuming Meself would demand the upper bunk, and silently looked down at the cold cement floor. Meself continued to stand by the cell door, refusing to face the inside of the cell, as if to deny its existence.

"This is like a never-ending nightmare," Youseff mumbled. "Maybe we've been here all along and what we thought was our earlier life is just an illusion, brought on by the beating. Maybe we really do have amnesia and can't remember how we ended up in jail."

Meself remained silent, contemplating the surroundings and trying to ignore the noise emanating from the other cells. Eventually he turned around to answer Youseff.

"No, I refuse to believe we're *supposed* to be here. Even though I'm unwilling to completely accept everything Paul was telling us about the Indians and their magical powers, one thing is for certain: When we came back out of that tunnel, we were stuck in a different place and time. I don't give a shit about how or why it happened; all I know is that our only hope to get back to where we came from is to get back into that damned tunnel."

"Paul says for us just to bide our time and we might get a chance to do that," Youseff concluded.

"But what happens in the meantime?"

Meantime, Pearl and Warden Peck were on their knees in his office, facing each other, silently praying their own personal prayers. When Peck heard Pearl mumble an 'Amen,' he reached over to her and grabbed her tiny clenched hands with his large fingers.

"What's wrong, Pearl? You appear to be troubled."

"Sometimes I worry about the well-being of the inmates," she admitted, keeping her eyes lowered, even though she sensed he was looking directly into her face.

"I see."

He waited for her to elaborate, but she kept quiet. He could feel her hands shaking and could see her face twitching. He knew she was hiding something.

"I see," he repeated. "Any prisoners in particular that you're concerned about?"

"No, not really."

"Are you sure?" he asked. "Because I could check if you really wanted to know. Plus, we could pray for them together."

"Well..."

"Yes..?"

"Well, there are those two brothers who were in the infirmary. I'm worried that they may have been released before they had completely recovered."

"Actually, our doctor gave them a clean bill of health and released them from the infirmary, but if it would make you feel better, we can ask the Lord to look over them and help make their transition back to the cell block as easy as possible."

"Do they face any additional punishment, I mean for the escape attempt?"

"I believe they learned their lesson when they surprised Wilkinson the day they popped out of the wall... Remind me to show you where the tunnel is sometime."

"Okay."

"Let us begin: Lord, please look over our wayward brothers who attempted to flee from this fine institution before their rehabilitation was complete. Please help show them the error of their ways and please protect them from any dangers or threats that they may encounter in this place. Help them heal completely from their injuries, so that they can continue to contribute to the operation of this facility and so that they can take full advantage of the educational opportunities available to them. And if they have yet to accept you, dear Jesus, as their personal Lord and savior, please help show them the light, whether that light comes from a fellow inmate, from a guard, from myself or from Pearl. I know that Pearl has shown a particular interest in the salvation of one of the brothers and we pray that she has been a positive influence on his soul. Please set Pearl's mind at ease concerning the welfare of this man, for we know that he weighs heavy on her mind. Her daily and nightly visits to this man have indeed been admirable and we pray that her time with this man has been well spent. She thinks of him constantly, Lord, perhaps to her own detriment. Please help keep Pearl's thoughts pure and help her not dwell on this incarcerated man beyond what you feel is necessary to ensure his salvation. Please give us a sign that Pearl's thoughts and actions remain pure, dear Lord, and that she has not been adversely influenced by any ungodly forces associated with this man... Are your thoughts pure, Pearl? Tell me in front of the Lord Jesus Christ, who we pray in His name, that your thoughts and actions have been pure, Pearl...Amen."

Before she could answer, she felt the warden take one of his hands from her clenched hands. She soon sensed Peck's fingers reach under her skirt, burrow between her thighs and squeeze under the crotch of her panties.

He leaned over to the kneeling woman and whispered, "You're wet, Pearl. You've allowed yourself to become sexually aroused about this man while I was sincerely praying for his welfare. You should be ashamed of yourself, Pearl. Feel shame for your sinful ways. For shame, Pearl. Shame on you."

Pearl sobbed.

***

On their first recreational period in the prison yard, Meself and Youseff were content to simply get some fresh air, taking a seat at a wooden table near the doors of the Main Corridor. Some of the other inmates milled around the yard, standing in small groups, often glancing over to the brothers as if they were the main topic of discussion amongst the men. Only a few inmates picked up mallets and busied themselves with physical activities.

"Where's the badminton court?" asked Youseff. "I heard talk that some of the inmates were playing badminton recently."

"Badminton? Are you kiddin' me?" Meself responded.

"That's just what I heard."

"So, were you hoping to join in or did you just want to place some bets?"

"Neither. I was just making conversation."

Youseff resigned himself to watching the couple of men with the mallets, observing them as they tapped their chisels against white sandstone grave markers. It was their job to carve markers for the Whitegate Cemetery, where a steady stream of dead inmates were carted and buried.

"Where's the croquet court?" asked Youseff. "I heard talk that some of the inmates were playing croquet recently."

A familiar growl was heard behind them and the brothers turned to see Paul pulling up beside them in his four-wheeled dog sulky. "I see you boys are surviving the lock-up."

"I guess you could call it that," answered Meself without looking down.

"Listen, I can't talk long because I think the screws are watching me pretty close, but I believe the escape plan is still in the works. You haven't said anything to anybody, have you?"

"Nope," declared Meself. "I haven't even updated my Facebook page."

"What?"

"Don't pay no mind to my brother," Youseff chimed in. "He's been a little down in the dumps lately."

"Yeah, being locked in a room that I can barely stand up in tends to affect me that way."

"Well, cheer up," announced Paul. "Like I said, there's still a good possibility we can break out of here. I was talkin' to this maintenance guy Ardie and he says the warden asked him to just put a lock on the hatch in the boiler room. They're apparently not destroying the tunnel – at least not yet, so time may be running out for us to pull this thing off."

"You gotta key to the lock?" Youseff inquired.

"Don't need one. Ardie says there's a fire axe in the boiler room beside the hose."

"So there's a fire axe that's easily accessible to the inmates?" asked Meself.

"Well, not really. I mean, it's in the boiler room, and it's behind emergency glass. And the boiler room door has a sign on it which clearly states 'Authorized Personnel Only'."

"Oh, that explains everything then," Meself commented, rolling his eyes for no one in particular to see. "Obviously, the fire axe is completely off limits to the prisoners."

"There's usually guards around that area too, though I don't expect there to be any nearby when we need to access the room."

"Just an observation," Youseff observed. "But it might be a good idea in the future for this Ardie guy not to tell many inmates about the fire axe in boiler room."

"Why?" asked Paul.

"Yes, Waugh," replied Youseff. "Ardie Waugh."

"No, I mean why shouldn't Waugh?"

"Why shouldn't Waugh what?" Meself asked, unable to follow along.

"Tell inmates about the fire axe," Youseff repeated.

"Why?" asked Paul.

"Yes, Waugh," replied Youseff. "Ardie Waugh."

Now the dogs were growling again, sensing Paul's growing confusion and frustration. "Listen, I gotta go. I'll keep in touch."

Meself turned to look at Paul. "Can you get a message to Pearl for me, to tell her I'm okay?"

"To be honest with you," Paul answered, "I haven't seen Pearl since you boys left the infirmary. I don't know where they're keepin' her."

***

Pearl sobbed.

"Quitcher belly achin', Pearl, I'm just fulfilling my promise to show you the tunnel where we captured your boyfriend," Peck explained.

"Please don't call him my boyfriend," sobbed Pearl. "I want to go back upstairs. This place is creepy."

"Pearl, Pearl, Pearl," Peck repeated, shaking his head with a dismissive frown. "You've got to learn to trust your mentor. You want to atone for your sins, don't you? Have you no remorse for your shameful conduct?"

"Yes, sir. Forgive me, sir."

"Follow me over here, dear. I want to show you something."

Pearl followed.

"Did you know that every Good Friday, the devout Christians of the Philippines recreate Christ's crucifixion – some of them actually allowing their hands and feet to be nailed to crosses?"

"I think I saw that in National Geographic or something."

"Of course you did; of course you did."

Peck instructed the woman to stand with her back against the wooden beam which had the manacles attached at the bottom and near the top. He stepped up on a concrete block beside the beam.

"Can you reach your hands up above your head?"

"Why?" she asked.

"I think a little recreation... er, re-creation, would do you some good. Maybe give you some perspective on things. Don't worry; I'm not going to drive nails into your hands. Remember what I said about trusting me?"

Pearl carefully raised her arms above her head, where Peck was quick to grab her wrists, pull them upward and snap on the upper manacles.

"Ow! That hurts!" she protested, lifting herself up on the tips of her shoes to relieve some of the pressure. "They're cutting into my skin. Please take them off."

"In a little bit," he said, jumping off the block and immediately kneeling at her unbalanced feet. "But I think we first need to remove this fine footwear that I bought for you last Christmas."

"Please don't."

Peck ignored her and slipped off the shoes one by one, leaving her dangling on the tip toes of one bare foot – and then the other. He had to tug her legs downward in order to secure the bottom manacles to her ankles, which caused her to shriek in pain.

"Oh god, it hurts!" she begged. "Please let me go. I repent of my sins. I promise I'll be good!"

"Hey, hey, hey, now," he responded, standing up to face her. "You're not acting very Christ like. I don't think Jesus begged 'oh it hurts' and 'I promise to be good'... wah, wah, wah."

Peck tapped with his hands across his suit jacket until he felt a bulge near one of the inner pockets. He reached inside to pull out a small roll of duct tape. He patiently pulled off a long gray strip.

"You can never have too much duct tape in the boiler room," he said.

Peck stepped back up on the block so that he would be high enough to tightly wrap the tape around Pearl's forehead and across her eyes, again and again and again. Pearl mumbled incoherently during the process.

He leaned over to where Pearl's right ear was located under the tape and whispered, "I know you can hear me, dear Pearl. If you really want down from here, you've got one chance to tell me all about those two brothers you befriended in the infirmary. I want to know exactly what they were doing in that hole and what they're still planning to do. Did you take them clothes and food in the tunnel, Pearl? How else were you helping them? Come clean, Pearl, if you really want forgiveness."

"I don't know anything, I swear," she cried. "God as my witness, I really don't know anything about the brothers. I certainly never helped them with anything. You must believe me..."

While she was babbling, Peck pulled a small metal device from his pocket which looked like a set of heavy wire dentures with the teeth missing. He twisted a small key-like object on the front, which widened the two sides like a robot jaw opening. He waited for Pearl to say something requiring her mouth to be fully open, and then plopped the oral speculum inside. He held the device in place with one hand, while he opened the metal jaws wider with the other hand.

Pearl's tongue began flailing silently inside her caged mouth, while saliva started dripping over her enslaved lips. Her opportunity to confess had passed.

Peck meandered over to place where the ladder and hatch were located and yelled upward, "Ready when you are, Wilkinson!"

Pearl was engulfed in darkness like, well, like a pearl in a mollusk shell. Because of the tape, she could barely hear, except when Peck's mouth was next to her ear or when he was yelling to Wilkinson. Her aching wrists and ankles added to her growing fear and panic. She began reassessing the amount of time she was spending as a volunteer at the prison.

A blast of cold water to the face forced the back of her head tightly against the beam, but the pain of the impact was quickly overcome by the realization that she drowning. A tsunami flooded her gaping mouth with such force that she could feel the fillings in her teeth break loose and follow the rush of water down her throat. Her tongue attempted to follow suit, getting twisted back inside her mouth with the tip tapping her uvula like a piñata.

She desperately tried to cough, but the incoming stream of water made it impossible. She could feel her stomach and her lungs filling up to the point of bursting. Now her teeth were starting to feel loose.

The excess water splashed down the front of her elongated body, soaking her clothes to the point where they clung tightly against her skin, revealing every contour of her figure. The thin blouse that she wore left nothing to the imagination once it was drenched.

"That's enough, Wilkinson," commanded Peck.

As soon as Wilkinson turned off the fire hose, Pearl began violently hacking and choking, forcing the invading water out of her weakened body. Water and vomit involuntarily gushed from her mouth, and she gasped for as much oxygen as possible in between the heaves. She resembled a half-drowned rat, covered in sewage and filth.

"She looks sexy as hell," Wilkinson observed.

"Yes, she is quite the temptress."

"Wouldn't it be great to get a bunch of college girls together, wearing T-shirts, and spray them with ice cold water? It could be like a competition. Maybe call it a Wet T-shirt Contest or something."

"I don't think society is quite ready for that kind of activity, Wilkinson. Most college girls I know have too much self-respect to participate in such frivolity."

"I guess you're right, the only girls who would be willing to participate in such a contest would be those drugged-up hippy chicks – and who wants to see them all wet? Although most of them could use a shower..."

Peck slowly walked over to the coughing and shivering Pearl, being careful not to get his shoes muddy. He fished for a penknife in his pants pocket and stepped up on the block.

"If you can hear me, Pearl, I'm going to cut the tape away from your head, and then we'll get you down from the beam so you can catch your breath. You're quite a mess. I just thought you'd like to know."

Peck cut the tape near the beam, freeing her head, but did not attempt to remove the sticky duct tape from around her hair and face. She felt his hand against her sternum, steadying her while he unlocked the manacles on her wrists. She would have fell on her face otherwise.

"Help hold her up, Wilkinson, while I unlock her feet."

Once she was free from the wooden beam, the two led her over to the curved bench in the center of the room. The relief experienced from the release of the sharp manacles was temporary, however, because as soon as she was lying stomach down on the bench she felt her hands and feet being tugged into the heavy metal devices once again.

Her arms, which had been dangling loosely over the sides of the bench, were suddenly taught as they were forced into the handcuffs. She heard the joints popping in her elbows and shoulders. Her wrists were still numb from the previous ordeal.

While Wilkinson was securing her ankles to the floor, Peck delicately removed the speculum from her mouth. The saliva and mucous-covered device popped easily from her swollen jaws. Peck tossed the nasty thing to the floor.

"There, you see, how merciful I can be, Pearl? With you lying there with that clamp in your mouth, I could have easily shoved my member down your throat and added a new protein drink to your liquid diet, but I care for you too much to do that. Besides, I wanted to give you another opportunity to tell me about those two brothers and how you've helped them."

Pearl would have confessed to anything at that point, but her jaws were locked, possibly broken from the force of the water, so all she could do was grunt and babble like a patient from the Trans-Allegheny Lunatic Asylum.

"So be it."

The next thing Pearl knew, Peck was cutting through the back of her blouse with his penknife, leaving her back exposed to the cool, stale basement air. She felt the knife tip scratch across the vertebra of her spine and would've cut across her bra if she had one on, but she was helpless to move out of the blade's way.

"Ready when you are, Captain Wilkinson."

Thick three-foot long leather strips slashing across the soft flesh of her back was not something Pearl was accustomed to, as was communicated by her gut-wrenching scream. Reflexes caused her arms and legs to jump momentarily but the sharp pain of the manacles quickly restricted her struggling.

"The Devil himself is deeply entrenched in your soul, Pearl, but we will do everything in our power to rip the demon out! Continue on, Wilkinson!"

Blow after blow after blow cut deeply across her back, the tips of the strap often curling around the right side of her waist and chest, biting into the tender flesh and leaving Pearl to dwell in a sea of anguish. More of the stagnant water that was still residing deep in her stomach and lungs now spluttered forth from her mouth, making her screams gargled and garbled.

Her mind was racing, panicked and distressed. She tried to think of more pleasant times, like when her dad took the family for cookouts at Oglebay Park in the summers of her youth, but then Pearl began identifying with the grill as soon as the next hot slash across her back was felt, violently interrupting her train of thought.

She felt blood pooling amongst the ribbons of flesh, and then stream off her back, following the direction of the welts and dripping onto the floor. Each strike also caused the blood to splatter up her neck and over her head... her head which was feeling very light... feeling very light... very light... very...

Pearl slobbered.

***

Every day Ellis Davis stood at the bars of his first-floor cell in the South Hall and watched in silence as a procession of fellow inmates paraded past him toward the open shower area. Ellis's cell was directly across from the white cement block wall which represented the community shower stall.

The cement blocks provided some semblance of privacy to the showering scoundrels, since the community shower heads were mounted on the side of the wall that did not face the cell block. But Ellis could still watch as the guards led each group in front of his cell, ogle the inmates as they disrobed before entering at one end of the shower stall, and then observe them toweling off as they exited the opposite end.

Ellis was getting quite the reputation among the other inmates, with some calling him the prison bird watcher, but no one ever said anything to his face because many believed he was already responsible for two unsolved murders within the prison. He also got a pass from the men on his floor, because when his group went into the shower stall, he appeared completely disinterested in them.

Ellis knew the procedure by heart, but he still watched the identical scenarios play out day after day after day, especially when the designated guard would pace in front of the row of disrobing inmates as they prepared to enter the stall. Some guards assigned to shower duty would conscientiously watch the inmates while they undressed, but others seemed too embarrassed to watch the strip show and opted to glance over to the cell block instead. These guards were the ones who would see Ellis standing at his cell door, staring through the steel bars, and they would usually give him a dirty look in return.

One day Ellis seemed hesitant to disrobe when it was his group's turn to enter the shower, but Ellis knew the guard wouldn't notice because that particular guard never looked at the inmates while they undressed. The guard would dutifully pace in front of the inmates as expected, but would always look away until the group had entered the stall. It was actually quite easy for Ellis to snatch the guard's large key ring and crack the man in the head with his own baton.

"Get dressed!" Ellis commanded of the other five men in the row. "We've got a prison to take over!"

Ellis knelt down to remove the guard's pistol, and then slapped the man's face until he regained consciousness. Ellis forced the man into the shower stall at gunpoint, knowing that the guards on the upper tiers of the cell block could not get a clear shot at him.

Ellis yelled back to his cellmate, Red Snider, who was standing just outside the shower stall, "Tell the guards above to drop their weapons and open all the cells on this block – or this man is going to die!"

Two of the five men in the queue for the shower seemed too shocked to get re-dressed and watched in awe as the scene unfolded. Ellis tossed the key ring to Meself, who fumbled the catch but retrieved the keys from the floor.

"I thought I told you fuckers to get dressed!" Ellis yelled. "Open the door to the hall with those and then lock us in once you're in the Main Corridor. Then you need to meet up with Paul in the Sugar Shack. He'll tell you what to do once you're down there."

Meself and Youseff scampered to get dressed, pausing only when they heard the steel bars snap open, releasing the inmates from all three floors of the cell block. Most of the men stormed out through the open cell doors, but some refused to participate in the uprising and remained in their cells to protect what little possessions they owned.

As the polluted sea of inhumanity converged in the shower area, bringing along a few more helpless guards with it, the John brothers took their leave and headed straight for the doors which led out to the Main Corridor. Trying one key after another until the lock finally sprung open, the boys scurried through the entrance and locked the door behind them. Alarm sirens began sounding as the two raced down the hall, both hoping they wouldn't encounter any resistance.

Paul was waiting as expected in the recreational room, alone in the dimly-lit space, except for his two work dogs. "You boys got the keys?" he asked as soon as the brothers appeared in the room.

Meself handed Paul the ring, trying to keep his distance from the snarling dogs near his feet. The piercing squeal of the alarm was obviously hurting the sensitive hearing of the dogs. They seemed desperate to get away from the noise.

"Before we go to the boiler room, we have to get Gene Jarvis out of the dark cell. He's gonna cover our tracks and make sure we make a clean escape," Paul explained, snapping the reins on the dogs so that they started moving out of the Sugar Shack.

Meself and Youseff followed Paul to the so-called 'dark cell,' where Eugene Jarvis was in solitary confinement, awaiting trial for killing a guard in October. A trustee named Billy Hale had witnessed the murder, but he was being kept under the protective custody of the warden, who used the man as a personal chauffer.

Eugene burst from his cell as soon as Paul located the correct key. The man was massive in size, his prison uniform having its sleeves torn off and its pants legs torn open to accommodate the man's monstrous physique. Yes, you could say he was a hulk of a man.

At the sight of the man, the dogs' pointy tails swished beneath their hindquarters and they commenced to whimpering and cowering. If the brothers had had tails, they would've joined the canines.

"Follow me!" Paul ordered, slashing the dogs into action.

Eugene followed close behind Paul, and the brothers picked up the rear. The boiler room was at the end of the hallway. The boiler room door was locked, but Eugene's bare foot kicked the metal door in like it was balsa wood.

Trustee Billy Hale performed other tasks for the warden, besides chauffeuring his fat ass around town. Hale was also an aspirin junkie, begging the warden to pick him up more pills every time Peck directed him to the pharmacy.

"HALE!" growled Eugene the moment he saw the frail trustee hiding behind a generator with a bottle of aspirin tipped to his quivering lips. "You're gonna need more than aspirin to stop you from feeling what I'm gonna do!"

Eugene kicked the squalling dogs out his way and stomped over to the shaking man in the shadows of the room. Hale's neck proved a perfect fit for Eugene's grip, the fingers of one hand encircling the circumference of the pencil-necked geek.

As Eugene was lifting the young man off the floor with one hand, Paul scooted beside the men, carefully avoiding the flailing feet of Billy Hale as he helplessly kicked his legs in the air. Paul slapped a silver lighter in the big man's free hand.

"Let's stick with the program, Gene," Paul advised. "You can deal with that rat later."

Eugene tossed Billy Hale across the room, slamming the man into the wall and knocking him out. Suddenly the sirens ceased and everyone seemed to calm down.

"Why was that fella even down here?" Youseff wondered.

"Never mind that," Paul answered. "I need you and your brother to spread out those rags in that box over there, and then I need someone to dump over that barrel of fuel by the generator."

Meself and Youseff began tossing oily rags across the floor while Eugene tackled the barrel. Gas guzzled from the tank like there was no impending energy crisis. Meself noticed the case on the wall housing the fire axe. He smashed the emergency glass with a rag-covered fist, almost tripping over the unraveled fire hose in the process.

Youseff was at the hatch and noticed that a hose was keeping the entryway ajar. "I don't think you'll need the axe," he called to his brother. "There's no lock on the hatch."

"I'm keeping it anyway," he said, approaching the hatch, "just in case one end of the tunnel is blocked off."

When all four conscious men were at the hatch, Paul instructed Eugene to help him and his dogs down the hatch, and then light the boiler room on fire. Meself was the first person through the hatch, navigating the ladder with one hand holding the axe.

Youseff followed his brother down through the hole, but ignored him once he was at the bottom, so that he could grab the dogs and Paul as Eugene lifted them down one by one. Once everyone was in the subbasement, Eugene closed the hatch on the protruding hose.

Eugene flicked open the lid on the lighter, spun the spark wheel with his thumb and tossed the flaming box onto the saturated floor. Hurrying toward the door, he remembered to grab Billy Hale by his afro and pull the man out of the burning room.

Out the room and into the hall, down the hall and into the solitary cell, Hale was dragged by his curly hair. Hale's clenched fist containing his prized aspirin bottle bounced against the cement floor. Once inside the cell, Eugene slapped his victim into consciousness.

"Rats git their necks wrung."

Before Billy Hale could respond, Eugene was kneeling behind him and was reaching under his chin. Eugene snapped Billy's neck with one twist. But he didn't stop there. Without losing his grip, Eugene gave the neck another twist until he was face-to-face with Billy's effaced face.

But he didn't stop there. Eugene continued to twist Billy's wiry neck until the dead man's head popped off, spraying blood like a geyser to the top of the cell.

Eugene stood up and pulled the decapitated body to the corner of the cell, setting it up like a display, as the gushing gore subsided. Eugene pried the aspirin bottle from Billy's death grip, opened the cap and dumped the contents into the dead man's severed throat. He then dutifully returned the empty bottle to Billy's hand.

Still not completely satisfied with the look of his creation, and wanting to make sure future rats like Billy got a positive message from his work, Eugene broke off the portion of the cervical vertebrae protruding from the torso, which used to connect to Billy's skull, and used the pointed bone fragment to stab the body numerous times, eventually leaving the neck bone sticking out of the chest cavity. Critics would then agree that the work did indeed represent "man's inhumanity to man."

Meanwhile in the subbasement, Youseff helped get Paul onto his cart and the dogs hooked up, as smoke began seeping down through the partly open hatch. Paul and Youseff weren't paying attention to Meself, who was standing in front of the busy men and had his back to them.

"Guys," whispered Meself to the men behind him. "Turn around and look at this."

Youseff and Paul twisted around to Meself's point of view, catching Wilkinson with his hand on his whip and catching Peck with his semi-erect cock in Pearl's ass. Peck and Wilkinson were so caught, as in so caught up in their debauchery, that they didn't notice the intruders at first.

When Wilkinson realized they had an audience, he dropped the leather strap and grabbed for his pistol. At first, Wilkinson aimed the gun directly at Meself, but quickly lowered the weapon when the arm holding the gun was ripped off by a flying axe blade. As the severed arm struck the floor, the gun inadvertently fired, sending a stray bullet directly into the ear of Peck, who crumpled to the ground in a heap of horror.

Having lost an arm, Wilkinson stumbled backward into the wall, spraying even more blood onto the walls and floor, mixing with the blood of Peck and Pearl. Meself ran through the shower of blood, retrieved the fallen axe, and cut Wilkinson down once and for all with a slice through the guard's throat.

Wilkinson instinctively grabbed for his throat with his remaining hand, wide-eyed at the slaughter unfolding upon him. Meself tugged the axe from the man's neck, sending the dying man tumbling to the floor.

"Don't worry; the doc has released you to go back to work."

Youseff was trying to loosen the manacles tearing into the wrists of Pearl, who was unresponsive on the wooden platform. "We don't have the keys!"

"I don't want to try to cut them off with the axe, in case I miss," Meself responded.

"Maybe the keys are in Peck's pocket..."

"Leave her!" yelled Paul, grabbing the flashlight tucked inside his shirt. "We've got to get through the tunnel!"

"We can't just leave her!" Meself countered. "The only other exit is on fire!"

"Well, you're not gonna use my cart to move her through the tunnel. I can tell you that right now. Leave her and maybe the fire crew can get to her before the smoke does."

Meself got down on his knees in front of Pearl's face and desperately whispered, "I don't know if you can hear me, but I'm sorry for all this. I know it's my fault. If we could take you with us, we would. I swear."

Moundsville's hall of pain
On the north side of hell,
I've spent the last six years
In a five by seven cell;
Moundsville's hall of pain
Where abuse and sorrow grow,
It's very hard to smile,
When pain is all you know;
Moundsville's hall of pain
A reflection of society,
Each time I look in the mirror
I see a lot of you in me.

-    Written on the wall: Floor 1 Block
A Cell 6

The greyhounds leapt out the exit of the tunnel, pulling Paul's cart through the air and ensuring a rough landing. The cart slammed onto the ground sending Paul careening across the darkened chamber, head over feet (if he had feet), while his flashlight flew from his hand and went out upon impact. The dogs padded over to their fallen rider and began licking the dirt from his face.

"Where's the fuckin' light?" Meself asked, emerging from the tunnel.

"I wanna know what happened to the cement wall," Youseff figuratively observed in the dark.

"Dammit dogs, get off me!" Paul yelled. "We gotta try to find that flashlight and hope it works. I gave my lighter to Gene."

The men began crawling around the room, except for Paul who was crawl-impaired, searching in the dark for the lost flashlight. Youseff crawled near the area where he heard the dogs gnawing and growling, but could only feel sticks and large rocks.

"Wait," announced Paul, "I think I found it. I knew it didn't go far. Let me try to get the damn thing on."

After screwing the loose lens back onto the top, the flashlight produced its beam and Paul directed it to the middle of the chamber. With the light, Youseff was

156

able to see what he had his hands on and he jumped away.

"Oh my god, it's a skeleton!"

The dogs continued to gnaw at the bones, until one hound successfully broke off a rib bone and began running to the corner of the chamber.

"Get that damn dog, somebody!" Paul yelled. "We need the skeleton to be intact!"

Meself chased the runaway dog with the help of the flashlight beam, while Youseff concentrated on pushing the other dog away from the remaining bones. Meself got into a tugging match with the canine, trying to pull the bone from its canines. When the rib popped from the greyhound's mouth, the dog immediately snapped at Meself's hand and barked in protest.

"You bite me and it'll be the last thing you do," Meself warned, waving the fire axe at the beast, and then turning to walk back to the center of the chamber. Before the light beam was redirected back to the skeleton, Meself noticed a small wooden door in the corner of the dirt-walled room.

Meself thought about seeing where the door led and leaving the others behind, but he felt obligated to return the bone. He tossed the recovered bone back into the heap big pile representing the Indian's rib cage.

"Why do we need the skeleton intact?" asked Youseff, who was sitting Indian style beside the bones.

"I'll show you why," Paul answered, "as soon as Meself picks me up and moves me to the skeleton."

Meself complied with the request and soon all three men were sitting around the collection of bones which once belonged to Adena Chief Tadach. The dogs were keeping their distance now.

Paul reached into his shirt pocket and brought out a palm-sized oval stone with inscriptions carved into one side. Most of the carvings were strange logographs, but a carving at the bottom appeared to be a stickman in repose, possibly representing the dead body of the Adena Chief.

"This is why we need the skeleton intact," Paul explained, showing the stone to the brothers by illuminating it with the flashlight. "This is the original Grave Creek Stone, which was unearthed at this site in the eighteen thirties. The original was thought to be lost, but secret societies have kept it hidden until I brought it to the Serpents Club."

"What do the three lines of symbols mean on top of the stick man?" Youseff asked.

"No one has ever interpreted the inscription," Paul explained. "No one until now, that is. There is no record of the language used by the Adena tribe, but many believe the language was similar to the Algonquin. I've been comparing the symbols on the stone to a collection of ancient Algonquin shaman chants, which my outside contacts obtained for me."

"And you've since written a scholarly thesis on your discovery for some prestigious archeological publication?" Meself sarcastically asked.

"Hell no!" Paul answered. "I've kept the discovery to myself so that I – and I alone – have the power to raise the dead!"

"Raise the dead, huh? Listen, Paul, if you don't mind, my brother and I would like to take our leave from this creepy hole in the ground. But if you want to stay behind and cast your little spells and black magic, you're welcome to do so..."

"You're not going anywhere!" Paul interrupted. "Consider yourselves lucky for being here with me. From what you guys have told me about where you came from, your knowledge is indispensible to me."

"Let's stick around, Meself," Youseff volunteered. "I'm curious about what'll happen with this stone and chanting stuff."

"Forgive me, but I still don't see the point in raising the dead – even if it were possible."

"The prison was built over another Adena burial place," Paul expounded, "so I'm assuming the raised spirit would wreak havoc on everyone occupying the sacred ground."

"You mean the men who just helped you escape? You want to 'wreak havoc' on those guys? Ellis, Red... Gene?"

"They helped us escape because they owed me for past favors. But we're all even now and I need to cover my tracks."

"Okay," added Meself, "so what about Pearl? Hasn't she had enough havoc wreaked upon her? You wanna wreak even more?"

"Not my problem."

"Not your problem?!" Meself repeated back, clutching the handle of the axe until his knuckles ached. "Not your problem?!"

"Oh, come on, the woman is already half dead. You know that. Fuggit about her."

Meself didn't understand why he felt such a strong connection to Pearl. Certainly she wasn't the first woman who gave herself completely to him, only for him to turn around and abandon.

Once the arguments had subsided, Paul placed the flashlight vertically on the ground, allowing the light beam to show on the ceiling. He cupped the stone in his hands (he would've gotten on his knees if he had any) and began to chant:

"Kit anamikon mani, mweckineckagoian kitcitwa oniciciiwewin; kije manito ki mamawiitim; kakina endactiwatcikwewak kin awacamenj ki kitcitwawinigo, gaie kitcitwawina jesos ka anicinabewiitisotc kiiawing."

Meself rolled his eyes, until he saw the vertical beam from the flashlight bend, arc and spin around the chamber, flashing light on all the walls and the participants, like some kind of cheap arena concert lighting from the 1980's. The two dogs huddled together near the small door, whining and whimpering at the bizarre light show. Youseff tried making shadow figures with his fingers.

"Kitcitwa mani, kije manito wekwisisimate gaganotamawicinam neta pataiang, nongom gaie wi nipoiang gaganotamawicinam."

Dust from the bone pile arose and swirled within the dancing light beam, turning the light into various colors of the spectrum. Meself crawled back away from the spectacle, stopping only when his back felt the cold dirt wall of the chamber. The dogs barked in fear. Youseff sneezed.

"Kekona ki ingi."

The dust-filled, color-flashing light beam wobbled and waved, causing an eerie vibration to emanate throughout the vault. Suddenly the bottom of the beam separated from the flashlight and continued to move upward toward the top of the beam, where it flashed and popped like a firecracker, causing the flashlight to fly across the room and almost hit the dogs.

Now only a bright orb of light, like a fertilized cloud, hovered in the air above the bones. The men watched in awe as the orb expanded and contracted, as if it were breathing. Trying to remain in control, Paul lifted a shaky arm and pointed to the tunnel. The orb spun and then swept itself through the entrance of the tunnel, leaving the chamber in darkness.

The men sat silently in the dark, as did the dogs...

"...Gee, it's awfully dark in here...and quiet too..."

The men continued to sit silently in the dark, as did the dogs...

"...Like I said, it's awfully dark –"

"– Shut the fuck up, Youseff!" blurted Meself, feeling his heart beating rapidly, painfully, within his chest. "We all know it's fucking dark in here!"

"But not so quiet now..."

"Okay, Paul, you've had your fun playing Mr. Wizard," Meself said. "Can we leave now?... Paul?..."

"Yeah, I'm here... If you can find the door and someone can help me find my cart and dogs..."

"I can get to the door," Meself answered. "Youseff, would you help Mr. Wizard find his stuff so we can get out of this hellhole?"

"Sure, no problem," Youseff replied, but as soon as he stood up and took one step, he got his foot stuck in the fragile skull of the skeleton. He lost his balance and fell onto Paul, who cried out in pain.

The dogs ran over toward their Master's voice, either concerned about Paul's well-being or afraid of Meself approaching them. Meself felt around in the dark until he located the door. He tried pulling and pushing the door from various positions, but it was securely locked from the opposite side.

"I hope there's no people or pets nearby, because I'm chopping through this damn door!"

Youseff and Paul could hear Meself swinging the fire axe into the small door, cracking the wood on many swings but thumping into the dirt on others. Cracks of barely visible light streaked through some of the gashes in the wood.

Meself dropped the axe and began pulling at the damaged wood until most of the door was torn away. "Oh shit, I think we're in the fucking museum!"

Youseff dragged Paul and his cart to the opening, where Meself was already crawling through. The dogs followed, still frightened of the unfamiliar surroundings.

Once everyone was on the carpeted side of the doorway, Youseff confirmed that they were indeed inside the Delf Norona Museum, specifically on the first floor. There were a couple of ceiling lights on, probably for security, but it was obvious that the place was closed. The men could also tell from the windows that it was dark outside.

While Youseff was helping Paul onto his cart, Meself said, "I guess we'll just go straight out the front doors."

A simple twist of the latch that connected the front doors released the locking bar and allowed the glass doors to swing open. After tossing the axe behind some shrubbery, Meself held the door open for Youseff and Paul.

"They really need better security around here," Meself observed.

"It's always easier breaking out of a place than breaking in," Paul replied as he and his dogs carted through the doorway and onto the sidewalk adjacent to Jefferson Avenue.

As all three men looked across the street at the imposing structure of the West Virginia State Penitentiary, lit primarily by the street lamps, Youseff added, "I think you're right."

No one seemed to take note of the cool night air or the absence of any other people or traffic, but Meself noticed an unexpected sight down the street near the main entrance of the prison. "Youseff, I think I see our van down there!"

"Let's go!" Paul suggested.

The men traveled down the street as fast as they could, ignoring the other vehicles parked in the visitor's lot. Youseff assisted Paul and the dogs into the back of the van, while Meself jumped into the driver's side, thankful that he apparently forgot to lock the doors.

Youseff climbed into the passenger's side, pulled on his seatbelt, waited for a few seconds, and then looked over to Meself, who was staring out the windshield. "What's wrong?"

"What's wrong?" Meself responded. "What's wrong is I don't have any fucking keys. That's what's wrong."

"Can you hot wire it?" Paul asked.

"I don't know how to do that shit!"

"If you got a screwdriver in here, I can do it," Paul volunteered.

"Maybe there's one in the glove box," Youseff said, popping open the small compartment in front of him and pushing some papers around. "Oh, look what I found, my extra set of keys!"

"Youseff, why would you keep our extra set of car keys *inside the vehicle*?"

"Because I know you never lock the van."

"Gimme the fuckin' keys, Youseff!"

Meself turned over the ignition and reached down to the shifter to put the van into reverse. He had to remind himself not to hurry, in order to avoid drawing any attention from anyone who may still be awake in the neighboring homes.

"Wait a second, Meself."

"What now?"

"What about our film? What about the ladies?"

"Fuck 'em."

"Yeah, fuck 'em," added Paul. "Let's go."

"We might have to forfeit our deposit," Youseff warned.

"We just escaped from another dimension and you're worried about getting a deposit back?"

"Well, it's more than just a deposit. I mean, we're trying to be a legitimate company, so we have to be careful about our reputation and all. If word gets around that we abandon projects and –."

"Okay, so what do you suggest we do, because I don't want to spend even one more second in this god-forsaken town?"

"Well, I mean, how long would it really take to go inside and…"

"Go inside? Youseff, if you wanna just *go inside*, you be my guest. You can catch up with me later down by the river, in Wheeling… just have one of the whores drive you."

"Fine! I will!"

Youseff unhooked his seatbelt, opened the door and jumped down to the pavement. He slammed the door shut and began stomping off in the direction of the prison entrance.

"Are you fucking kidding me, Youseff?" Meself mumbled, turning back to look at Paul. "Is he fucking kidding me?"

Meself rolled down the passenger side window. "Youseff, get back in this fucking van! Youseff, don't go in there! I'll leave; I swear to god, I'll leave you behind!"

With his brother barking behind him, Youseff continued to march to the lobby doors of the prison. He'd never felt so independent, so free, in all his life. A look of determination crossed Youseff's face as he heard the tires of the van squealing onto the street.

My brother shouldn't be drawing attention to himself, thought Youseff.

***

Star Blaze used her natural tracking skills to find Joy exploring the prison's wood shop. Much of the equipment in the shop was still present, but the machinery showed obvious signs of disrepair and neglect. Decades old saw dust and boards littered the peeling white-washed room.

"So here you are."

Joy was slightly startled by Star's sudden appearance. "Yeah, I was just exploring a little until shooting resumes. I think I was the only cheerleader in high school who actually liked shop class. Are the boys back yet?"

"Not as far as I know," Star answered. "So this is the wood shop? I wonder if any of this stuff still works."

"Well I was able to turn the lights on, but I was afraid to touch anything else."

Star walked up close to Joy and embraced her, cupping the redhead's jean-laden butt cheeks with her hands. "Are you afraid to touch me?"

Joy returned the favor, reaching her hands behind Star. "Does this answer your question?" she smiled.

Star leaned her head down until the two women's foreheads touched, sending heat waves through both of their bodies. They looked into each other's eyes, catching their own reflections in the irises.

Star whispered, "I didn't tell anyone else this, but that thing you did with the eggs turned me on big time. I'm thinking of adding something like that to my routine at the club."

Star began kneading the bottom of Joy's cheeks, opening and closing the cleft near her butthole. Joy purred in response and Star began kissing her befreckled neck.

"You tryin' to limber me up, so I can break my own record?" asked Joy between sighs.

"Maybe, but I know a way to really loosen up your tight little ass."

"Show me, Indian girl, because you've got me in the mood for just about anything."

The two kissed immediately, open-mouthed and wild-tongued. Star was the first to break the embrace, leaving Joy standing with weak knees in the center of the room and wanting more. Star walked to a scrap pile of wood in one corner and picked out a one-inch thick board which was about a foot and a half long and a half-foot wide.

"Nothing makes you limber like a nice piece of lumber."

Star brought the plank over to a rusty ban saw and placed it on the saw table. She looked around the vertical piece of machinery until she found the power switch on the back column. The thing screeched to life.

"Come over here Joy."

Joy was afraid of the screaming, squalling machinery, which was nothing like the high tech tools she used in high school; but was also curious about what Star had in mind. Joy approached the rumbling ban saw.

"Make me a nice paddle that I can use on your ass," Star instructed.

"I-I-I can't…" Joy stammered.

"Why not?"

167

"I don't have any safety goggles."

"What?"

"Safety goggles. You're not supposed to use dangerous machinery like this without safety goggles."

"You're not in high school, you know that don't you?"

"It doesn't matter. What if I get a wood chip in my eye?"

Star strutted over to some cabinets and began opening them in a flurry, one by one, until... "Ah ha!"

Star waved a pair of hard plastic goggles at Joy and carried her find back to the spinning ban saw. The goggles were covered in dust and grime, causing Joy to sneer as soon as she saw them.

"Come on now," encouraged Star. "I'm sure you've had worse things on your face. Any more excuses and I'll have you put some holes in the paddle with the drill press."

Not having a template or a penciled guideline to go by, Joy surprised herself by the symmetry she was able to attain by slowly feeding the board into the rusty blade. While cutting a perfect handle at the bottom, Joy worried that the old blade could snap at any time and cause her to lose a finger or even chip the polish of her expensive manicure. But Joy conquered her fears enough to complete the job by rounding off the top corners.

Joy picked up the paddle, blew off the saw dust and handled the implement to Star.

"Nice job!" Star exclaimed. "Now put your hands on the edge of the saw table and bend over."

"Shouldn't we turn this loud thing off?"

"No, I don't want anyone hearing you yelp while I'm beating your ass."

"Maybe we shouldn't do this. I've still got some nude scenes to shoot. The boys'll be pissed if my butt is bruised up."

"Quit your whining," Star chastised. "I'll let you keep your shorts on. Besides, the guys know how to film around stuff like blemishes. Plus, a little powder or makeup will cover anything up. Now bend over like I told you!"

Joy complied, being careful to keep her fingers away from the whirling blade in front of her. Moments after bending over, she felt the first stinging crack of the paddle on the back of her jean shorts.

"Aiyee!" she screamed, her voice barely rising above the rumbling din of the saw.

Joy tightened her grip on the edge of the saw table, preparing herself physically and mentally for the next swat… *Crack!*

"Oww! Dammit that hurts! Please take it easy!"
Crack!

Joy's ass felt like a dry sponge which was having every ounce of moisture squeezed out of it and the wetness being directed down into the depths of her pussy, which contracted and convulsed with each swat from Star.

Crack!

Now Joy was beginning to feel lightheaded, the constant hum of the saw and the steady pounding on her ass were slowly putting her into a trance-like stupor. *Crack!* Her body was submitting more and more to a superior force with each successive blow. *Crack!* Joy could vaguely perceive a strange aura surrounding her as she attempted to see through the thick, dirty lenses of the goggles. *Crack!* She felt she was engulfed in a white cloud of shimmering fog. *Crack!*

A sudden tug on her hair brought her back to reality. She thought she heard the wooden paddle hit the floor. Two hands were felt on her head and her face was being forced toward the saw blade, its hum echoing louder and louder in her ears, like the ominous sound of a crashing waterfall when a drifting raft approaches the precipice.

Joy brought up her own hands to try to pry the invading pair from her head, but Star's fingers were locked tightly around the sides of Joy's head. If Joy could have turned around, the sight of Star's glowing eyes, flaring nostrils and gnashing teeth would have frightened her to death. At least that would have been an easier way to die.

Joy initially felt strands of hair on the top of her hair get caught up and pulled into the ban blade. She usually passed out at the first sight of even one drop of blood, but why wasn't she fainting now? She prayed that she would just black out.

The spinning blade dug into the top of her forehead, spraying blood across her safety goggles and into her mouth as she tried to scream. She stayed conscious until the blade hit the bone, slicing into her brain tissue, showering her aggressor with torn hair, skull fragments and gore.

Star held the dead girl's head to the saw table until she was completely scalped. After the job was done, Star allowed the body to drop to the floor while the bloody red scalp remained on the platform.

***

Jennie Dagmaar busied herself in the kitchen, where she felt comfortable in a very stereo-typical way. She was also hungry, so she searched through the cabinets to see if there was any leftover food that the prison tour guides may have left behind. She had passed on the eggs earlier in the evening.

And she sang whilst she searched:

> *Cocino en la cocina.*
> *Cocino en la cocina.*
> *En la estufa, con la olla.*
> *En la estufa, con la olla.*
> *Yo lavo en la cocina.*
> *Yo lavo en la cocina.*

A door behind her creaked open and she quickly glanced behind, catching a quick glimpse of Star. She returned her attention to the cabinets, but stopped singing.

"Star, you embarrassed me," Jennie pouted without turning around. "I don't like to sing to an audience... I'm seeing if maybe, just maybe, I could find a snack to hold me over until shooting continues."

Jennie didn't notice Star's blood-covered clothing when she initially looked back, but as Star approached her from behind she began to pick up on a nauseating scent which quickly helped her to lose her appetite. She snarled her nose in disgust.

"What *is* that smell?" she asked, turning completely around to face Star.

Star immediately wrapped her sticky fingers around Jennie's throat and squeezed. Jennie felt her eyes popping forward from the immense pressure being applied to her throat, meeting Star's vacant, glowing stare in the process. Jennie tried reaching up to grab Star's hands, but the effort was useless and she soon passed out from lack of oxygen.

Star dragged Jennie's limp body over to a large machine labeled as an industrial meat mixer. The machine looked like a three-foot high chest freezer with a lid on the top. Star lifted open the lid and pushed Jennie's head into the box with her left hand. She used her right hand to grab a large crank on the side of the machine.

As Star turned the large crank, wide blades began spinning inside the machine. The grinding sound of the whirling blades caused Jennie to stir and awaken, but only long enough to witness her face and head being forced deeper and closer to destruction. Rather than attempting to defend herself, Jennie now used her hands to cross herself and accept her destino.

Jennie continued crossing herself even as she felt her face being churned into mincemeat. She also found it impossible to scream when the metal met the mandible and maxilla. The blades thumped relentlessly against her thick skull, turning the massive machine into a macabre organ grinder.

Star's grip on the back of the young woman's head was both merciless and manifest, while her durability and determination was doubly demonstrated by her ability to continue cranking the machine through the gristle. The bottom of the mixer filled with a meaty concoction that the government would be reluctant to serve school children on taco day.

– Federal Dietary Guidelines advise consuming protein from a variety of sources, and recommend weekly amounts from three Protein foods (formerly lean meat and beans) subgroups: (1) seafood; (2) meat, poultry, and eggs; and (3) nuts, seeds, and soy products. The proposed meal patterns contain weekly and daily amounts of meats/meat alternates, but do not specify amounts for subgroups introduced by the Dietary Guidelines. Consumption of a balanced variety of protein foods can contribute to improved nutrient intake and health benefits. –

Once Star's diet of destruction was achieved and Jennie was sufficiently scalped and scalloped, she let go of the crank and allowed her victim's body to dangle and quiver at the side of the mixer, like a pollo with its cabeza cut off.

***

Virginia Foxxx was resting on the cot inside the holding cell of the museum area, still trying to recover from the power play executed on her body while she was strapped to the nearby electric chair. She was a heavy sleeper, so she didn't notice when Star entered the museum room.

Star walked past the holding cell and headed straight for a glass case on the wall, which served as a display for confiscated shanks and other homemade weaponry. Without regard for her own well-being, Star smashed the glass with her fist and selected the longest, thickest, sharpest, most ominousest blade she could find.

The shattered glass caused Virginia to jump up in the cot, frightened from her sleep by the sudden crash. She looked over to see Star standing in a pile of broken glass.

"Star! What the hell are you doing? You can't be breakin' shit like that. What's wrong with you girl?"

Star slowly turned around with the shank clutched in her hand and her eyes blazing bright white light, like lasers aimed at a police helicopter.

"Oh shit!" Virginia yelled as she leapt up and closed the wire-fenced door of the holding cell, snapping shut an antique padlock from the inside, and not caring whether a key existed for the lock or not.

Star marched over to the holding cell, still staring directly at Virginia as the pent up prisoner cowered in the farthest corner of the cell. Star shook the door of the cell, but couldn't get it to budge.

"You get away from me right now with that knife," Virginia commanded. "You hear me? What'd I ever do to you anyway?"

Star walked around the sides of the cage, trying to determine if she could reach her victim with the blade. She tried shaking the door again, but was still unsuccessful. Star dropped to her knees in front of the cell door.

"You can't get in here, so go away. Take your knife and leave. Nobody wants you around here."

Star slowly tilted her head back and opened her mouth. In moments, the light emanating from her eyes dissipated and her body began to shimmy and shake. If she had been naked, her garter would've immediately been filled with dollar bills.

Star's head shook violently, causing spittle to fly from her open mouth. Sounds of gargling and moaning came from deep within her body. Virginia thought the woman was going to explode right in front of her.

"You are fucked up, girl. I mean really fucked up!"

Suddenly a white orb of light, about the size of a goose egg, burst forth from Star's mouth and hovered over her head, spinning and vibrating.

As soon as Virginia opened her mouth to say "Oh my," the orb swept through the cage and jammed itself into Virginia's big mouth and down her throat.

"...God," Virginia gulped, coughing, hacking and trying to force the entity from her invaded body.

Soon Virginia was the one with the glowing eyes and the agenda. Virginia stood up and walked toward the door of the holding cell. She held her hand out to Star on the other side of the fence. When Star pushed the shank through one of the links of the fence, Virginia grabbed the weapon, and then fell to her knees.

Grinning at no one in particular, Virginia placed her left hand on top of her head and brought the blade up to her forehead with the other hand. With great precision, Virginia began cutting away at her scalp from front to back, like she was slicing a loaf of bread on her head. Blood began streaming down the sides of her face and head as she continued to cut away more and more of her skin, smiling with satisfaction during the scalping.

When Virginia finally sliced through the back of her head, she lifted the bloody scalp with her left hand and brought it in front of her face. She began to laugh hysterically at the mangled clump of skin and hair, but soon fell face first onto the cement floor.

Star saw the shank drop against the cage and was able to retrieve it through the fence, while Virginia started another round of coughing and hacking from her position on the floor. Blood continued to seep from Virginia's head, flowing under the fence and surrounding Star's stained knees.

Star sucked the white orb back into her own mouth as soon as it emerged from Virginia's lifeless body.

***

As Youseff approached the front doors of the prison, he immediately realized that all the lights were out in the lobby. He expected the doors to be locked, even though there were plenty of cars still in the parking lot. The doors swung open when he pushed on them.

"Hello? Hey, is anyone around? Hello?"

He felt around the wall inside the doors until he located a light switch, which lit the empty quiet room. He walked directly to the door leading to the Main Corridor, so that he could go inside the nearby guard room and retrieve his camera.

Finding the camera was no problem, since the combination lock was still in place and Youseff remembered the combination, which he had set up to match their box at the downtown Wheeling post office.

Satisfied with the recovery of the camera, Youseff decided it would be better to follow his brother's example and abandon the set. But the closer he got to the front doors, the more guilt he felt for not checking on the cast.

"Dammit," he mumbled to himself. "Let me see if I can find out what's going on around here."

He walked back to the guard room where there was still one flashlight on a charger. He popped the flashlight off its base and headed out into the darkened halls, keeping the camera close to his side.

***

After searching for the girls and finding only dead bodies, Kay panicked and began shutting off the lights, hoping to shield herself from the gruesome sights and perhaps hide from the killer. She knew the John brothers had been going back toward the Sugar Shack during the break, so she headed there with flashlight in hand, looking to rendezvous with the filmmakers.

Upon reaching the recreation room, she also turned the lights off in the basement, and then sat quietly in the corner near the hallway – waiting, waiting for Meself and Youseff. She listened intently for any indication that someone was approaching, but could only hear her own heavy breathing. She tried to breathe more quietly.

Piercing the darkness came two glowing disks, moving like eyes attached to a floating body. Kay stopped breathing, holding her breath so as not to attract attention. She feared the eerie presence of the stranger, especially since she had not heard any sounds like footsteps prior to the entity's arrival. The mysterious eyes seemed to be scanning the dark room, selectively illuminating the room with narrow laser-like beams of light.

Kay bit her bottom lip, worried she would cry out or gasp in fear. She tried to make herself smaller, pulling her legs up in front of her and clutching them with her arms. But the eyes still found her. She knew they would.

Kay flicked on her flashlight and was presented with a vision of Star, bloodied and bedeviled, a knife in her hand and boldly approaching. Kay scrambled to her feet and ran down the hallway, quickly ducking into the first sturdy door that she found and locking it behind her. She found herself in the boiler room.

Using her flashlight, Kay desperately looked for another door or a way to exit from the dark room, knowing that it wouldn't be long before Star gained access. Kay noticed a hatch on the floor, but the lid appeared too heavy to lift. It didn't look like there was any other way out and Star was already kicking hard at the door.

Spurred by the steady stomping against the door and the curdled creaking of the wood frame, Kay rushed to find something, anything, which she could take refuge behind, even though hiding had not worked for her earlier. She tucked herself behind the generator just as Star broke through the door.

Like oncoming headlights viewed from afar as a vehicle spins out of control, Kay watched the glowing *eye beams* of Star speed around the room. From ceiling to floor, no part of the room went unsearched by Star's roaming eyes. Kay resigned herself to hiding her face in her hands and praying to a god she never trusted nor fully believed in.

The spiritual act of prayer seemed to draw Star to the generator, where she stood silently beside the huge machine. Star's eyes reflected their light off Kay's smooth scalp.

After a few minutes of dead silence, Kay forced herself to peek out between her fingers to ascertain her fate, which was standing directly over her with the shank raised high and ready to strike. There would be no opportunity to seize this fate by the throat.

Kay found it odd that Star's figure appeared to be backlit, making her pursuer appear almost shadow-like, except for the glowing eyes.

"What the fuck is happening here?!" Youseff demanded, turning on the ceiling light in the process.

Star spun around to face Youseff, keeping her knife raised in the air, and marched straight toward him as he stood in the doorway. When he saw her approaching with the shank, he jumped back into the hall. Star's speedy approach and exit from the room was hampered by Youseff tripping her on the way out, sticking his leg out as soon as she crossed the threshold. Star careened across the narrow hallway and stumbled into the wall.

"Help me!" screamed Kay.

Youseff rushed into the room and immediately looked for the presence of the fire axe. He was thankful to see the tool was available, but he had to smash the glass case in order to retrieve it. By the time he placed his camera and flashlight on the floor, and had the axe firmly in hand, Star was re-entering the room and seemed even more determined to use her blade to scalp everyone present.

Youseff rushed straight at Star, swinging the axe in circles above his head, knowing that his weapon of choice had a longer reach advantage than the shank which Star clutched in her hand. As he came within striking distance, he made sure he looked away from the mesmerizing eyes of the femme fatale.

Once again, Star was sent careening head first into the hallway, but this time her body didn't follow. The glowing eyes of the severed head, as it rolled into the dim hall made it look like a loose disco ball. Inside the boiler room, the headless body of Star slashed aimlessly with the shank as she tried to regain her balance like an embarrassing outtake of John Travolta from "*Saturday Night Fever*."

Blood spurted from Star's neck, making the floor slippery and causing the walking corpse to stumble toward the generator. Kay screeched in fright at the sight of the body falling toward her, still slashing with the knife as if it sensed where Kay was hiding.

"No, you don't!" yelled Youseff, as if a headless body could hear.

Youseff ran up behind Star and sank the axe blade deep into her back, and then pulled the bloody torso away from the cowering Kay. Tugging the axe from her back, Youseff watched as the body continued to writhe on the floor, spinning in its own blood and still waving the knife in the air.

Startled at the sight in front of him, Youseff was shocked further when he heard Star's voice behind him from the hall. The severed head, missing its voice box, was warning, "Youseff, stop trying to save the little bitch! The cunt is mine!"

Youseff forced himself to regain composure, while his mind raced for a solution to his undead dilemma. Sacred words began to flow effortlessly from his mouth:

"I adjure you, Satan, enemy of man's salvation, acknowledge the justice and goodness of God the Father, who by just judgment has damned your pride and envy – depart from this servant of God, whom the Lord has made in His own image, adorned with His gifts, and has mercifully adopted as His child!"

The headless body quit spinning and slashing, but began using its hands and knees to rise up again. As soon as the body was back on its feet, it walked toward Youseff, shank in hand.

"I adjure you, Satan, prince of this world, acknowledge the power and strength of Jesus Christ, who conquered you in the desert, overcame you in the garden, despoiled you on the Cross, and rising from the tomb, transferred your victims to the kingdom of light!"

The body of Star stopped suddenly and dropped its arm, allowing the knife to fall onto the blood-soaked floor.

"I adjure you, Satan, deceiver of the human race, acknowledge the Spirit of truth and grace, who repels your snares and confounds your lies – depart from this creature of God, whom He has signed by the heavenly seal; withdraw from this girl whom God has made a holy temple by a spiritual unction!"

Star fell forward, onto her knees, and then crumpled completely to the floor in front of Youseff.

"Leave, therefore, Satan, in the name of the Father and of the Son and of the Holy Spirit; leave through the faith and the prayer of the Church; leave through the sign of the holy Cross of our Lord Jesus Christ, who lives and reigns forever and ever. Amen!"

The body finally became still. The eyes in the dismembered head in the hall also went dark.

"*I believe* I killed her," Youseff quietly announced. "You can come out now."

"Can you turn out the light so I don't have to see it?"

After turning off the light switch near the doorway, Youseff heard the woman sobbing. He walked toward the crying Kay, but tripped over Star's blood-gurgling body. Kay screamed when she heard Youseff stumble, afraid that he was now going to fall on her with a blade in his hand. The axe blade bounced off the generator, barely missing Kay's skull, but Youseff was able to twist his body into the nearby wall and ended up sitting on the floor beside Kay.

"I can't seem to stop tripping over dead bodies," he joked.

Not that she was ever in the mood for jokes, but Kay definitely wasn't amused at that particular moment by Youseff's lame ass attempt at macabre humor. Kay could dress maturely and act tough most of the time, but an ordeal like the one she just went through really brought out her youth and vulnerability.

"They're all dead, you know," she managed to say through her sobs. "Joy, Virginia and Jennie... Star killed them all, and then she came after me."

Youseff placed the axe on the floor between them. Kay still had her flashlight at her side, but didn't want to turn it on.

"Why didn't you call the authorities?" Youseff asked.

"Ha! Stupid me had to collect all the girls' cell phones at the beginning of the production, because I didn't want anyone's phone ringing during the filming. They balked about turning them over, but did after I agreed to put mine away also. I hid them in one of your grip boxes."

"Well, I guess it's the thought that counts."

"Yeah, I'm just so damn thoughtful. I'm starting to think karma is finally coming around to bite me in the ass. But I'm no worse than anyone else I know, including my fucking family. I'm beginning to believe there is not one good person in this whole West Virginia northern panhandle. After awhile, I just gave up on people and figured if I can't beat them, join them, you know?"

"I don't qualify as a good person?" Youseff asked. "I just saved you, remember? I could've walked away and let Shankawajea there carve you up like a Thanksgiving turkey. Come to think of it, today is

Thanksgiving, so maybe we should be thankful for our blessings."

"Yeah, right, I've learned that people usually have their own selfish reasons for doing things for others. So, sorry, if I don't kiss your fat ass in gratitude for all you've done for me, especially since I wouldn't even be here if it wasn't for you and your sick twisted brother."

"Oh, Kay."

"Don't *Oh-Kay* me. You sound just like my goddam mother. She liked to act all nurturing and understanding too, but as soon as company or family left, she'd lock me in a fucking closet for no reason. She was pretty young when she got pregnant with me and she treated me like I was robbing her of her childhood or something."

"I'm sorry to hear that. My childhood wasn't exactly all guns and roses either. Both my parents died when I was young and my brother took it upon himself to raise me, even though we were the same age."

"Well, thankfully, I wasn't raised solely by my mother or my absentee dad. She dumped me off on my grandmother after I became too much of a burden. But I didn't complain, my grandmother was a saint compared to her evil spawn of a daughter. Grandma always acted like a whore and a slut, but at least she never locked me in a closet. Those years with Grandma Pearl were the best of my life, but then she died from a blood clot when I was thirteen and I was sent straight back to mommy dearest."

"Pearl, you say? Your grandmother's name was Pearl? That's…an interesting name."

"Yeah, in fact she used to work right here at the prison as some sort of volunteer. My god, the stories she used to tell me..."

"I can imagine."

"Yeah, well, just as I was telling you earlier, there are no good people in this part of the world. Everyone has an agenda. My Grandma left the prison on a hospital gurney, after she was brutalized and tortured during a riot. I guess she was almost dead when paramedics found her."

"I'm guessing you didn't know your grandfather."

"Hell no; typical man," she said. "My mother once told me the prison warden got Grandma pregnant, but Grandma said the warden was the most impotent man she ever knew. So it must have been someone else."

"Well, maybe you'll find out who your grandfather is someday," Youseff added. "Hell, I just found out recently I had a great niece."

When it appeared that Kay no longer wanted to talk, Youseff took the opportunity to tell her all about his wonderful ideas for zombie movies. His zombie flicks would break the mold of typical zombie fiction and take the genre in new directions. He treated her to a verbal description of one gory scene after another, even though she had just witnessed enough gore to last a lifetime.

After a few moments of uncomfortable silence while Youseff was catching his breath, Kay pressed a button on her wrist watch to light up the lens. "I bet dawn is breaking," she said. "That tour guide is going to be arriving soon."

"I don't think we should be around when he arrives. I also don't think we need to go back upstairs and take the chance of bumping into him."

"Well, what do you suggest we do? We're in a prison, remember? There's not too many ways out of here."

"I bet I know a way," he answered, "and I think it'll work out for us now that I've got the spirit world sort of under control. Come on out of there and follow me."

Youseff walked over to the hatch in the floor and opened the lid. He then retrieved his flashlight and camera as Kay inspected the entryway.

"You want me to go down there?"

"I'll go first, if you'll shine your flashlight for me," Youseff volunteered. "I've got to carry my camera down and I don't want to drop it."

Youseff tucked his flashlight inside his belt and dropped the axe down through the hole. Kay positioned herself to light up the path forward/downward for Youseff. He easily navigated the rungs with his free hand.

Once Youseff was on the floor of the subbasement, he placed the camera at his feet, and then used his flashlight to light the way for Kay. He tried not to look up Kay's long black skirt as she entered the passage, but he failed miserably.

The entry to the tunnel looked the same as when Youseff and his brother entered it during the break in production. Kay was shaking her head before Youseff even showed her the inglorious hole.

"No way," she said, shining her flashlight into the void. "No fucking way am I going in there."

"It's not so bad once you get in there. Come on, I'll help you along."

"I said no fucking way am I going into that fucking tunnel. Did you not hear me telling you about the hours I was forced to spend in dark closets? I'm fucking claustrophobic and I am not going in there. Period."

"Well, I can't leave you here."

"Why the fuck not? I can take care of myself. You go ahead and do your spelunking, or whatever you call it."

"What about the guard upstairs? What if the police are already up there?"

"Then I'll act like the little victimized female, too scared to talk and too traumatized to remember anything. I'll be all right."

Youseff managed to hold his flashlight and the axe handle in one hand and his camera in the other as he began to climb into the tunnel. "Good luck then, maybe I'll see you on the other side."

"If the pigs are upstairs, I'll try to stall them so you can get through," she concluded, turning away from the tunnel.

Youseff had his hands full, literally, even without the female tagging along. It was slow going for him as he inched along, trying not to drag the camera in the dirt. He tried putting the flashlight in his mouth. He tried using the pick side of the fire axe to dig into the dirt in front of him and pull himself forward. He tried everything he could think of to make better progress through the tunnel. He finally took off his shirt, wrapped the camera inside, and tried pulling it along beside him.

When he finally reached the end, he was faced with the same cement block wall that he and his brother had originally encountered. Taking the axe firmly in hand, he mumbled, "I'm not going back this time."

Redheads and blondes
Boats and fast Vettes,
Got my Candy Apples from Compton
Got my tickets in on my bets.
Said my lawyers are on standby
And my friends are nowhere to be found,
They got me on CNN
And my picture up all over town.

- Written on the wall: Floor 1 Block B Cell 9

Amy considered herself to be a good person, but then again she wasn't from the Wheeling-Moundsville area. Amy was a healthy young woman in her mid-thirties, who had worked for the West Virginia Division of Natural Resources for many years, usually being shuffled from place to place, wherever they needed her, because of her perpetual single status.

Amy didn't mind being transferred from state park to state park at a moment's notice, because it gave her the opportunity to see and experience the entire Wild and Wonderful State of West Virginia. Actually, she thought of herself as rather wild and wonderful, with her beautiful brunette hair matching perfectly with her dark brown state-issued uniform. Her DNR hat was especially cute on her.

But this evening, she had the rather tame and tedious task of serving as an unarmed night watchman at the Delf Norona Museum. She made the best of the situation, however, by bringing along a large book called *"True West Virginia Ghost Stories."* Consequently, she sat at the reception desk with her feet propped up on the desktop and her attention focused on the book.

Only the sound of something scraping across the floor was able to break her concentration. Rather than get up from her comfortable position, she opted to stay seated since the sound seemed to be getting closer. No one else was supposed to be in the facility. Amy closed her book and placed it on the desk.

After a short time, a bare-chested middle-eastern-looking man carrying a cloth bag in one hand and a blood-stained axe in the other came limping into the lobby, heading straight for the glass doors. He limped from what appeared to be a skull attached to his foot.

The man was startled when he realized there was someone observing him. He looked at her and said, "Good evening, Miss."

He continued his lumbering and laborious trek toward the door. Amy was amazed that the intruder was going to just walk out the door, dragging a broken skull with him. Plus, it was cold as hell outside and this guy didn't have a shirt on.

"Excuse me," Amy spoke up, but was promptly ignored. "I said, *excuse me, sir.*"

Youseff stopped just inside the doorway and turned around to face the reception desk. "Yes? How may I help you, Miss?"

Amy removed her legs from the desk and stood up behind it. "Oh, I don't know. Maybe you could begin by explaining your presence here at the Delf Norona Museum in the middle of the night, especially since you have a skull stuck on your foot, an axe in your hand and god-knows-what in your satchel."

"Satchel?"

"The bag in your hand."

Youseff looked down and said, "Oh, that's just my shirt."

"Well, why don't you leave your axe there by the door and come over and sit by me."

"You're not gonna call the cops, are you?"

"Not unless you give me a reason to," she said, motioning to a chair beside the desk. "But if you walk out that door, you can bet your ass I'll be on the phone."

"Okay, okay, I'll come over to chat, but I can't stay long," he replied, leaning the axe against the door frame. "I've got some business to attend to."

Amy sat back down behind the desk, while Youseff hobbled over to the chair adjacent to the desk and plopped down. Obviously exhausted, he grabbed his right ankle and pulled up his leg to rest on his left knee. Amy watched as he began tugging at the large skull attached to his shoe.

"I believe this is yours."

Youseff twisted and pulled at the skull until it popped off his shoe. He triumphantly slammed the artifact onto the desk, scattering ancient teeth across the desktop. Youseff glanced at Amy's name tag.

"Amy meet Chief Tadach – Tadach, this is Amy," he announced.

"I'm more interested in who you are."

"Oh, me? My name is Youseff. It's nice to make your acquaintance, Amy."

"Likewise."

"It looks like you have a very fascinating job here, Amy."

"Well, tonight it is."

"I don't seem to remember a guard here the last time I visited the museum."

"A DNR officer was assigned here at night following a break-in a couple months ago."

"A break-in, you say?"

"Yes, coincidentally, it was on the same night as the massacre in the penitentiary."

"Massacre?"

"Certainly, you heard about the Thanksgiving Eve Massacre. I thought everyone in the state knew about it. A bunch of prostitutes were carved up. In fact, one was chopped up with an axe just like the one you were carrying."

"All this happened a couple of months ago?"

"Yep, Thanksgiving. I don't really know much more about it, since I didn't pay much attention when it happened. I'm not from around here, like I said."

"Um, Amy, do you mind me asking you what day it is today?"

"Sure, it's Ground Hog Day, February the second. In fact, in just a couple hours, French Creek Freddy should be giving his prediction for an early Spring at the Game Farm."

"Sometimes I think I'm living in the West Virginia bizarro version of the 'Groundhog Day' movie. You know, the one with Bill Murray."

"Yes, I'm familiar with the 'Groundhog Day' movie."

"I love Bill Murray," Youseff expounded. "I don't care whether he's playing a groundskeeper in 'CaddyShack' or a Ghostbuster in, well, in 'Ghostbusters.' The guy's a riot. Hey, did you know, he and his brothers used to caddy when they were younger? I kid you not. Him and his brothers even have some kind of restaurant in Florida called Caddyshack. Yes, they do, don't look at me like that, Amy. My info comes straight from Wikipedia and the iMDB. I mean, don't get me wrong, '*Garfield*' was a bit of a disappointment, but most of his other work is absolutely stellar. How about that cameo in '*Zombieland*,' wasn't that awesome? Classic Bill Murray there. But I'm still on the fence about '*Ghostbusters Three*.' I mean, it's gotta be better than '*Ghostbusters Two Electric Boogaloo*,' but there's no way a '*Ghostbusters Three*' could live up to the original. I guess they proved that with '*Ghostbusters Two*,' so why bother?"

"I don't believe I've seen '*Zombieland*'."

"Oh, you gotta see '*Zombieland*'! I love zombie movies. George Romero is like my idol. By the way, did you know I am a filmmaker? My camera is what's rolled up inside my shirt. Yeah, I'm hoping to create like the ultimate zombie flick, if I can convince my brother, that is."

Holding up the book she was reading, Amy replied, "I'm more into the supernatural than zombies. You know, ghosts and stuff."

"Well, if you had witnessed what I just experienced over in the prison, you'd believe in zombies too, I tell ya."

"I didn't say that I don't believe in zombies. I just said I prefer reading and researching the supernatural. In fact, I'd like to write about my experiences some time. I saw this horror writer give a speech at the West Virginia Book Festival about his books and he really inspired me. I even picked his brain after the marketplace closed. I've been reading everything I can get my hands on about the supernatural in Appalachia, hoping to get a good idea for a book. Since you're a filmmaker, maybe we can collaborate on something?"

"Well...what if I told you... Oh, never mind. I've really got to go."

"Tell me what? Tell me what?" she begged, leaning toward Youseff with an excited look on her face.

"I really shouldn't tell anyone about this."

"Hey, you can trust me. I didn't call the police when I saw you hopping through here, did I?"

"Well, what if I told you that I witnessed the so-called Thanksgiving Eve Massacre and that it most definitely involved the supernatural?"

"Oh...my...god..."

"And what if I also told you that I just came from there through a tunnel which led directly into Chief Tadach's burial vault?"

"You mean you hid in the tunnel for two months?"

"No, I wasn't in the tunnel for two months. Well, sort of. No, no, no, I wasn't in the tunnel for two months. When I entered the tunnel it was Thanksgiving, and when I exited about a half hour later it was apparently Groundhog Day. The tunnel is like a worm hole through time, affected by some kind of supernatural force from within the burial mound."

"Oh-my-god, oh-my-god, oh-my-god ... This is just the kind of story I've been waiting for! What do we do next? Let's go back through the tunnel!"

"There's no way I'm going back into that godforsaken tunnel. Right now, I've only missed like two months of my life. I think I can get back up to speed once I find my brother."

"Do you know where he is?"

"Maybe, I mean, we didn't like make plans to meet anywhere specific just in case one of us got lost in time or anything. The only problem is, I don't think I have the transportation to find him."

"Yes you do! Let me close up shop and we'll go find your brother!"

"But aren't you like abandoning your post?"

"No one knows when I leave in the morning. Besides, Youseff, I now consider myself a writer – and not some desk jockey for the State of West Virginia, by god!"

Although he put his shirt back on, it was a cold eleven mile ride up to Wheeling on Route 250. Amy's Jeep Wrangler had a cloth top which fluttered in the frigid morning air, allowing blasts of breezy bleakness to seep through the seams.

While waiting for the Jeep's motor to heat up enough to provide some warmth, Amy probed Youseff on the details of the Thanksgiving Eve Massacre, which she considered more significant than the story behind Pocahontas County's infamous Skull-Fucking Day. Youseff cautiously answered some of her questions, trying not to implicate himself or his brother in anything which could land them back behind bars. Amy assured him that she knew how to fictionalize the events in such a way that no one would get in trouble.

"The names will be changed to protect the guilty!" she joked.

"Get in the left lane and take the twenty-sixth street exit."

"You guys have a place down here?"

"No, we live in a van down by the river."

"That is *so* fucking cool!"

It didn't take long to find 23rd Street, but the white van was not down by the river. Youseff left the Jeep to inspect the area for tire tracks or telltale trash, but saw neither. He found himself staring across the Ohio at the Wheeling Peninsula Casino, mesmerized by the twinkling lights.

Amy startled Youseff when she walked up from behind. "Where to now?"

"Hell if I know. Maybe we could try the Serpents Club, but I doubt anyone is there at this time of the morning."

"Serpents Club – That is *so* fucking cool!"

"Yeah."

"Looks like the casino is open over there."

"You feel like playin' slots or something?"

"No, I was just making an observation," she observed. "A writer has to be very observant, you know."

"Hey!" Youseff blurted out. "I know something we could do. We could go to the post office and I can check my box. I should be able to tell if my brother has been there recently by how much mail there is."

"Is the post office open?"

"Not the service window, but the lobby area with the boxes is always open."

Amy stayed on Youseff's heels once they arrived at a post office on Chapline Street. The John brothers'

197

box was pretentiously large and featured a small combination lock instead of a keyed lock, which suited the brothers just fine since they both had a habit of losing keys.

Youseff had to use both hands to carry the large pile of letters to the desk in the center of the empty lobby. His brother had obviously not picked up the mail in weeks. Youseff began skimming through the envelopes.

"Damn, I hope those aren't all bills," Amy commented, still being observant.

"Actually, we don't get a whole lot of bills," Youseff answered, trying to concentrate on the return addresses.

"Living in a van...," she added.

Youseff paused when he got to a large white envelope and immediately began tearing it open. It was specifically addressed to him, which he found particularly peculiar.

"... down by the river," she concluded.

"I got something from the Appalachian Film Festival," he announced while pulling a stack of papers out of the envelope. "Dear Mr. Youseff John, We are pleased to inform you that the submission committee has reviewed your entry and approved it for inclusion in this year's Appalachian Film Festival competition. Your submission is eligible for consideration in the following juried categories: Best Film; Best Young Filmmaker; and Best Screenplay."

Amy listened closely as he read the top page. "Oh wow, congratulations, Youseff."

"Yeah," he responded while thoughtfully looking up to the ceiling, "too bad I don't remember submitting anything."

"Well, maybe this is part of that 'catching up' you said you had to do," she suggested. "Anyway, when is the film fest?"

"Would ya believe this weekend in Huntington?"

***

After searching in vain for the van and discovering the Serpents Club crudely boarded up, which was probably a violation of the Historic District zoning ordinances, Amy drove Youseff to her apartment so that she could pack up some clothes for the trip to the film festival. Youseff had no clothes to pack.

While Amy was packing, Youseff attempted to load the video from the camera onto her iMac desktop computer. He ended up watching and listening to a lot of gray static emptiness, which was reflected in the blank expression on his face. Amy entered the small living room with a suitcase.

"What's that?"

"It's supposed to be the footage I shot at the prison. I don't know what happened to it."

"Maybe that weird tunnel you were telling me about had some kind of magnetic field which erased all the video. You didn't back it up?"

"Where was I supposed to back it up? There was nowhere to back it up."

"Chill out. I thought maybe you had a laptop or something."

"Nope."

"Well, you must have used something to create your zombie movie, because it's closing the festival on Sunday night. Boy, you must be excited to see your film for the first time, especially since you don't remember making it."

Amy switched places at the computer desk with Youseff in order to make two reservations at the Holiday Plaza Hotel on Third Avenue. The festival was being held at the Keith Albee Orpheum on Fourth Avenue, so the Holiday Plaza was an ideal location. She could have stayed with a friend just outside Huntington, but Amy wanted to be right where the action was so that she could continue acquiring information for her book.

Youseff busied himself in Amy's refrigerator, worried that some food might spoil during their trip if he didn't eat it right away. He was also worried that Amy would ask him for a credit card to book the rooms.

"Adjacent rooms booked!" she announced.

Youseff entered the living room chomping on some cold pizza. "Thanks, Amy, [chewing] I'll pay you back if I win an award at the festival [chewing]. My credit card got stolen back in the seventies [chewing]."

"Gee, maybe you'd better report that."

"Yeah [coughing]," he agreed, choking on an anchovy.

***

Youseff had only been to Huntington once when he was a little kid. His parents took the young brothers to Camden Park. Youseff's most vivid memory of the amusement park was when he rode the Haunted House ride with his brother. Meself pushed him out of the car halfway through the ride and he had to find his own way out of the dark attraction without getting electrocuted or hit by other cars.

He ended up getting in trouble for not keeping his hands and feet inside the car at all times. The embarrassed family left the park soon after the incident.

Youseff had never been in downtown Huntington and was glad that Amy was driving, especially since a Marshall University basketball game was just letting out and a thundering herd of spectators were pouring into the streets. They had made good time traversing the state from north to south, only stopping once at a thrift store so that Amy could find some bizarre clothes to make Youseff look like a trendy filmmaker.

As they were entering the theater on the chilly evening of his movie premiere, Youseff felt overly warm in his heavy brown Dexter Blazer sports jacket (price $2.00) and felt overly itchy in his olive Tyne Crew Neck Sweater (price $1.00). He also felt flushed by his companion's sheer white skin-tight body suit, which stretched down over her perfectly-proportioned tits, across her petite waist line, and continued down to just barely cover her impressive ass (price $300).

Youseff offered her his jacket, since the sweater was more than enough for him, but she refused, silently insisting that the other festival attendees get an eye-full of her cold-activated nipples. Amy seemed to believe that the Academy Awards ceremony had moved to the Keith Albee Orpheum in Huntington, West Virginia.

The Keith Albee Orpheum was built in honor of the birth of Edward Albee in 1928. Edward's father had intended to name his newborn son "Keith," but pressure from his wife and in-laws caused him to reconsider and name the boy "Edward." Unfortunately, the marquee had already been constructed using the name "Keith Albee" and it was decided as a cost-saving measure to leave the marquee as it was. The construction had already cost over two million dollars.

Seating up to 3,000 *paid* patrons, the Keith Albee Orpheum exemplified the aristocratic and shabby chic culture of the 1920s with a Mexican Barrios design style. The crystal chandeliers, multiple balconies, vast cosmetic rooms, decadent smoking lounges, and cozy restroom fireplaces were all designed to mock and humiliate the people who would be most affected by the economic downturn of the late 1920's. The first production presented at the theatre in 1928 was a whimsical vaudeville musical by Mort Kennedy entitled, "*Kill the Poor*."

But the night Youseff and Amy presented their guest passes at the box office, the marquee proudly announced: Appalachian Film Festival Presents / ZILF – a film by Youseff John.

A movie poster for "*ZILF*" was also on display in a case near the entrance. The poster depicted the interior of an empty cell, along with the following prose written in blood on the cell wall:

> *Adjusting pupils*
> *To the harsh lighting*
> *Flashing inside; and*

Adjusting prior
To the harsh fighting
Flailing outside... her.
Nasty naked zombie zeotropes,
Scratching, slashing, stabbing
Hands and teeth in the
Screaming, slumping, struggling
Man in terror... his...
Pain upon pulse-stopping
Popping pain upon non-stopping
Pain upon pain
Upon pain.

"Where's the paparazzi?" Amy whispered as they snaked their way through the crowded lobby, her arm interwoven with Youseff's arm.

"Let's try *not* to attract the attention of the press," he answered nervously with a forced smile on his face.

"Why not? This is our, I mean, this is your big night, Youseff."

"Yeah and what if they ask me something specific about the film, which I haven't seen yet?"

"Just say, 'No comment'," she answered. "The press are used to hearing 'No comment.' Don't you watch the news?"

Youseff wanted to stop at the snack bar to pick up some popcorn and sour watermelon gummies, but Amy convinced him that he was representing filmmakers that evening and should not allow himself to be confused with common audience members. Besides, she knew she would have to pay for the treats.

Inside the theatre, Amy recommended that they sit toward the front, and for Youseff to take an aisle seat, which would benefit him if he were to be called up on stage during the awards ceremony. "You don't want to look clumsy climbing over a bunch of people."

"Yes, Amy," he said. "You know, you remind me a lot of my brother."

When the houselights came down in the half-filled theatre, Amy cussed a big guy sitting in front of her because he still had his cell phone light on. Youseff hoped the guy wouldn't turn around and punch him since Amy was his guest. After one last 'LOL' text, the man quietly turned off his phone.

For the next eighty-nine minutes, Youseff stared at the screen with his mouth agape, mesmerized by the images flashing before him. He felt like Little Alex DeLarge from "*The Clockwork Orange*," but he didn't need any mechanical device to keep his eyes wide open. If he had had popcorn, he would've choked on it.

Amy kept elbowing him, sometimes painfully, every time she saw a scene she liked. The audience in general was reacting to various scenes just as Youseff would expect them to, but thankfully they kept their elbows to themselves.

"I love the zombie girls," Amy whispered. "Where did you find them?"

"How the fuck should I know? I've never seen these chicks before in my life."

"Well, I hope they're not offended that you didn't invite them to the premiere."

The guy in front of Amy twisted his head around a bit and shushed her while she was midsentence. Amy kicked the back of his seat. "Don't shhhh me, cell phone boy."

"You know, I just don't understand this," whispered Youseff, leaning over closer to Amy so as not to further disturb the man. "It just doesn't seem like my camera work and editing, but it does look like something I'd write... If my name wasn't on the film as screenwriter, I think I'd sue whoever claimed to write it."

When the last of the credits rolled, featuring names he was unfamiliar with (except for his own, which appeared numerous times), Youseff was astounded to hear applause from the audience. Amy prolonged the praise by rising to her feet and looking around to shame others into a standing ovation. The applause increased, but it may have been in appreciation for Amy showing off her ass.

A few audience members followed Amy's example and stood up while they continued to clap their hands. Youseff actually felt embarrassed by the adoration; especially for accepting praise for work which he didn't recall creating. In fact, he felt like a politician.

The applause continued as the audience transferred its attention to festival chairman Chuck E. Clair, who walked out on stage as the movie screen retracted toward the ceiling. Stagehands rolled out a podium, along with a table of colorful glass Blenko apples, from the opposite side.

"What? A standing ovation for me?" he joked once he was behind the podium microphone.

Bada-Bing.

"I guess that last flick proved that zombie girls don't just eat brains."

Bada-Bing.

"I heard the working title for *ZILF* was originally '*I'm a Zombie from Kentucky and I Like Bukkake*'."

Bada-Bing.

"But seriously, we may not all agree when it comes to my poor attempt at humor, but I think there's one thing that we all can agree on – and that's the quality of films we've all enjoyed at this year's Appalachian Film Festival. I do believe this is the best collection of full-length movies and short films we've ever featured at the festival."

Clair paused to allow for some lukewarm applause to subside.

"Yes, our judges had a difficult time arriving at a consensus for this year's award recipients. But I have the envelope right here. If you hear your name announced, please come up on stage and accept your Blenko."

Youseff managed to keep his composure throughout the ceremony, having to listen to a litany of lame laments from the winners of the categories leading up to Best Film, specifically, Best Micro Film: "*Appalachian Intellect: An In Depth Look*"; Best Short: "*Will Little Timmy Get to Eat Today?*"; Best Documentary: "*The Jesco White Campaign – Dancin' My Way to the* White *House*"; Best Screenplay: Hasil Lilly for "*I'm My Own Grandpa – An Appalachian Love Story Set to Music*"; and Best Young Filmmaker: Mimi Knoll for "*Wrong Turn 5 – Five Wrongs Don't Make it Right*."

After the Best Young Filmmaker accepted her Blenko and her $250 check and gave her little liberal spiel at the podium, Chuck E. Clair announced, "And now, the moment you've been waiting for – the prize of one thousand dollars for Best Film at this year's Appalachian Film Festival goes to... Youseff John for '*ZILF*'!"

Youseff was half asleep when he heard his name called. He stood up while the audience was clapping, looked over at the row of gawking people to his right and decided to squeeze past all of them, even though the path to the aisle on his left was clear. Yes, he stepped on a lot of toes that evening, but no one was more agitated than a mysterious couple seated in the mezzanine.

After accepting the bright red apple from Clair and shaking the man's hand, Youseff found his way to the podium. He placed the glass apple on top of the podium and held a hand up to his brow to shield his eyes from the stage lights. There was a lady in red in the mezzanine vigorously waving to him.

"Thank you all. I entered '*ZILF*' in the festival this year because I'd heard that apples were being given away as prizes. Of course, I was thinking of laptops and not glass fruit."

Youseff found it difficult to keep his train of thought. He was no longer shielding his eyes, but he was pretty sure the lady in the red tank top was now flashing her tits at him. Instead, he directed his attention to Amy in the lower level seats.

"I'd like to especially thank my new friend Amy for accompanying me here this weekend and providing support. I wish that my brother could be here, but I'm not sure where he is exactly. The last couple of months have passed so quickly. I must have been very busy, obviously. I'm just glad that you all enjoyed the movie and I hope to provide more interesting films in the future. Thank you!"

He raised his glass apple in the air, prompting the audience to respond again with applause. He covered his brow with his free hand to take one last look at the mezzanine, but now couldn't see the lady in red. She had vanished like a ghost.

Upon returning to the Holiday Plaza, Youseff and Amy celebrated with drinks in the bar. Youseff insisted that they order drinks which had a color similar to his translucent red apple award. The bartender tried his best to recreate the color, using a vanilla liqueur, bourbon, cherry schnapps and Big Red soda. Amy paid.

When the bar became crowded as the evening wore on, Youseff said he was tired and wanted to retire to his room before anyone recognized him. Amy was looking forward to having a few beers, instead of the "Big Red Beemkos" she had to endure with Youseff, so she told him goodnight and explained that she was going to stay in the bar for awhile.

Amy thought about driving over to see a friend who lived near Camden Park, but realized it was too late and she was too inebriated to drive. Fortunately, she was not too inebriated to continue drinking, as she ordered quite a few drafts.

Just when she thought she'd get through one evening in a bar without getting hit upon, a shapely woman in a red leather skirt and a red halter top asked if she could sit in the bar stool next to Amy.

Amy welcomed the fortyish, middle-aged lady, amused by the squeaking sounds that the leather skirt produced against the cushioned bar stool as the woman wriggled onto the swivel seat for a little wiggle room. Wriggling and wiggling was apparently her specialty, but choosing a hair color was not. The woman's unnatural burgundy punk-like hair color, unsettlingly matched her burgeoning halter top and burdensome skirt.

"Your outfit matches the mixed drinks I was having earlier," Amy commented.

"Oh yeah, what were you drinking?"

"Something the bartender made with Big Red soda."

"I think I'll pass on that, unless I get drunk and I start to worry about spilling my drink. My name is Ruby."

"Of course it is," Amy laughed while lightly shaking the curvaceous woman's boney hand. "My name is Amy."

"Are you in town for something special or do you live around here?"

"I came down for the Appalachian Film Festival. A friend had a movie submitted. It actually won Best Film."

"I'm in town for the film festival too," Ruby replied. "I think I saw you sitting beside the guy who got up to get that apple thingy at the end. He won for that zombie movie, right?"

"Yeah, his name's Youseff."

"You mean like the children's charity where the kids take the little tubes around to your house and collect donations?"

"Ah, sort of, I guess. Are you thinking of UNICEF?"

"Yeah, yeah, that's it! Hey, isn't that Uniceff guy from Wheeling?"

"Yes, Youseff hails from the Wheeling area."

Ruby ordered a boilermaker from the bartender, consisting of a light beer and a shot of Jack Daniels.

"Looking to get wasted too, I see," Amy observed.

"Maybe, plus I like to collect shot glasses from the bars I visit. I noticed this place has their name engraved on the glasses."

Amy watched as Ruby dropped the shot glass into the beer mug and proceeded to drink the entire concoction down without taking a breath. Ruby slyly smiled at Amy, and then looked down to unsnap a small faux ruby-encrusted purse. Ruby did a quick half spin on her bar stool so that her back was to the bar. Amy twisted around in her chair in time to see Ruby open her purse, bring it up to her chin and drop in the empty shot glass from her mouth.

After the chaser, Ruby cut to the chase. Looking back at Amy as she snapped her purse closed, Ruby asked, "So, you wanna go upstairs to your room and fuck?"

"Sure, I guess," Amy answered, letting the liquor do the talking.

"And can you cover my drink, hun'?"

Amy suspected that her flirtatious friend did not have her own room at the hotel and she hoped that Ruby wasn't a prostitute, because that would be illegal. Plus, she didn't intend to pay for lesbian sex with a woman who was at least five years older than her.

Ruby expressed her intention of jumping in the shower as soon as Amy opened the door to the room, but Amy insisted on using the bathroom first since she had been drinking all evening. Ruby graciously agreed to wait.

While Amy was taking a piss, Ruby redded through her ruby red purse until she found her cell phone. Using her cloth tank top, she wiped a layer of sticky beer film off the case and jammed the phone between her ample breasts, hiding it from sight. She also made sure the phone was on vibration mode in case someone was to call while Amy was nearby.

"It's all yours," Amy announced as she exited the bathroom. "It looks like there are plenty of towels. I'll grab a quick shower once you're done."

Ruby left her purse on the dresser, since it only contained a shot glass and a razor, and sashayed into the bathroom, closing the door behind her. Amy sat down on the edge of the bed and turned on the television.

Inside the bathroom, Ruby quickly undressed and turned on both the shower and the sink faucets full blast. She speed-dialed her boyfriend, Robert "Little Codfish" Bricker, Jr.

Like his father, Robert "The Codfish" Bricker, Sr., Little Codfish worked for the organized crime syndicate in Wheeling. In a time where DNA can convict a man beyond a reasonable doubt, Little Codfish had learned from his father how to safely kill a man via vehicular manslaughter, using just a pair of driving gloves and a stolen car. The Wheeling boss had sent him and Ruby down to Huntington to find Youseff John before the police caught up to the missing filmmaker.

"Bobby? Are you there?" Ruby whispered into the phone.

"Yeah, where you at? Niagara Falls?"

"No, I'm at the Holiday Plaza on Third. I'm in a bathroom and I've got the shower running. Anyway, I think I found Uniceff."

"I thought he wasn't registered there."

"He isn't, but I believe his girlfriend may have booked the room."

"So are you in *his* bathroom or what?"

"No, no, no, I'm in his girlfriend's bathroom. They're not sharing a room. But I'm gonna try to find out from her where Uniceff is."

"Okay, but be careful. Call me if you need me. I'll be nearby."

"Toodles."

After a steamy shower, Ruby emerged from the bathroom, semi-wrapped in a towel which couldn't quite handle her curves. The hot dampness of her reddened skin helped the terry cloth cling. She also had a towel wrapped around her wet hair.

"Your turn, hon'. I left you a towel, but not much hot water."

"That's mighty red of you," Amy joked. "I guess since you had to take your outfit off, you thought you'd better scorch your body red."

"I'm one hot momma," Ruby responded. "You'll find that out once you're done in the shower."

When Amy was done with her shower, what she found was Ruby lying naked on the bed sheets, her breasts jutting toward the ceiling and jiggling like jello as she giggled at something on the television. Amy tossed her wet towel onto the floor beside Ruby's pile and joined her friend in bed. The TV was then turned off, but that was the only thing turned off in the room.

"You gulping down that boilermaker turned me on," Amy confessed as her hands caressed Ruby's body.

"I've got my own little boilermaker going on," Ruby invited. "You should get between my legs and taste it."

"M-m-m-m-m," she murmured, deciding to take the long way to the watering hole.

Amy began by suckling Ruby's red nipples, squeezing the breasts tightly together with her hands so that she could quickly switch her attention from one nipple to the other. Ruby's hands searched for Amy's breasts and pulled them up toward her hungry mouth as soon as her fingers made contact. Amy's tongue left the engorged nipples of her lover as Ruby pulled her torso upward.

The experienced mouth which had captured the shot glass earlier, latched onto Amy's left breast and almost sucked the whole thing in. While Ruby's uvula tickled Amy's entrapped nipple, the older woman's tongue lapped around every inch of breast meat that it could touch. Amy cooed at the pressure and stimulation being applied to her boob. She could also feel Ruby's jagged teeth on her delicate flesh, but that only served to excite her even more.

Ruby soon moved to the other breast and sucked it in, but continued to massage and knead Amy's left breast with her hand. As soon as Ruby released Amy's right tit, their lips met in an urgent wide-mouth kiss where the dueling tongues battled for position.

Amy's petite tongue proved no match for Ruby's muscular mouth organ. Ruby sucked hard at Amy's tongue, licking the underside with great strength and pulling it up forcibly from the bottom of Amy's mouth. Amy's tongue was a prisoner in another woman's mouth and she had no choice but to serve out her sentence.

Like a curious child who can't help touching a hot pan, Amy reached down between Ruby's legs where she felt uncontrolled heat emanating from Ruby's late-model oven. Ruby's thighs closed in around Amy's hand, making it hard for Amy to stroke with her fingers inside the inner folds of Ruby's slick canal. Amy had hoped the attention she was paying to Ruby's nether region would prompt Ruby to release her sore tongue, in anticipation that Amy's tongue could better serve her elsewhere.

The silent entreaty worked. Ruby released Amy's imprisoned tongue, sending it south to her labor camp on route sixty-nine to complete its sentence. As soon as Amy encircled Ruby's body, spreading her legs over Ruby's face, she dug her head deep within the grip of Ruby's thighs. Amy placed her hands firmly on Ruby's thighs, realizing too late that she probably couldn't pry the woman's legs from around her head even if she tried.

Even though Amy's tongue still throbbed with pain from the previous exercise, she slipped it into Ruby's well in order to taste the sweet nectar inside. The moment that Amy's tired tongue was encased in Ruby's inner sanctum, Amy felt Ruby's vaginal muscles capture and pull her tongue even deeper inside. Simultaneously, Amy felt her clit get sucked painfully inside Ruby's tireless mouth.

Amy felt like she was being devoured at both ends with no means of escape. Resistance was futile as Ruby's control became brutal; causing Amy's panicked body to finally collapse onto her tormentor in total submission.

Amy knew the only way she would be released from the older woman's grip would be to satisfy Ruby completely. Consequently, she took a deep breath, breathing in Ruby's aroused aroma through her nostrils, and garnered enough oral vigor to begin moving her tortured tongue inside Ruby's snare. Ruby's muffled moans could soon be heard under Amy's hips.

When Ruby's thighs increased their hold on Amy's head, Amy could no longer hear the moans but knew Ruby's climax was building. Soon Ruby's body was quaking and her vagina erupted in spasms, blending its squeezed juices into Amy's mouth. Amy took the opportunity to withdraw her tongue and nose from the grindstone.

Although her tongue was exhausted from the workout, Amy still found the energy to lick the sticky moisture from around her lips as she changed position to find Ruby's breasts once again. Sacrificing her own satisfaction, she yanked her crotch away from Ruby's mouth and clamped her own mouth back onto Ruby's breast. Now it was Ruby who was too spent to resist.

As Amy sucked and licked Ruby's warm tits, she was surprised to find that Ruby's body must still be in the throes of higher plateaus. Ruby's breasts vibrated and hummed under Amy's busy mouth.

Ruby suddenly sat up, knocking Amy away from her chest. "Hold on, hon'. Let me see who this is."

Ruby reached a hand between her sweaty breasts and pulled out her cell phone. She looked at the caller's number on the screen and flicked the power off. "It can wait," she announced to her flustered bedmate.

"Are you serious?" Amy asked. "You brought your cell into bed with us?"

"I never leave bed without it," Ruby smiled.

"If you hadn't noticed, I had the courtesy not only to put my cell on the bed stand there, but I also turned mine off."

"I see that," Ruby responded. "But you need to settle down, because it's now my turn to do the driving. So lie on your back up here on the pillows."

Amy tried to calm down as she crawled up beside Ruby and relaxed into the wet spot in the sheet where the older woman had been. Ruby's right hand stroking her pussy quickly calmed the beast within Amy.

Amy closed her eyes, enjoying the soft feeling of fingertips as they probed and petted her personal space. The pleasure made all her concerns and worries melt away and she began to purr in response. But then she felt the smooth, hard sensation of something pushing at the edge of her slit.

"What's that?" Amy breathlessly asked, barely audible.

"Don't you worry, honey," Ruby whispered from above, bringing her left hand to rest on Amy's forehead. "Mommy knows what's best."

"Mommy?"

"Yes, dear, Mommy's here to take care of you. You are the apple of my eye."

"You're not my mother," mumbled Amy.

Amy felt the smooth object slide into her pussy, but her spirit was too broken to resist. Ruby continued to rub her labia after the object was securely tucked inside. Sitting on her knees adjacent to Amy's vanquished body, Ruby twisted around backward to grab Amy's cell phone from the bed stand.

"Of course I'm your Mommy. I'll prove it to you."

Ruby flipped open the phone with her free hand and tapped the keypad with her thumb.

"Here, dear," Ruby said as she placed the phone into Amy's hand. "Just hit the send button so you can call home."

Amy didn't even need to open her eyes to follow Ruby's direction, since she was used to her phone and often used it without looking at it. Amy tapped the green button as requested.

Moments later she felt strong vibrations within her pussy while Ruby stroked her clit with more passion. "Oh god," Amy blurted out.

"Welcome home, dear," Ruby replied. "I'm so glad you called."

Amy tried to push the red button to disconnect the call, but Ruby snatched the phone from her hand. "Now, now, now, young lady, mommy knows what's best," chastised Ruby.

The vibrating within and the friction without was driving Amy to the point of no return. Her body was trembling like a dam about to burst. "Damn, damn, damn...."

Amy forgot where she was, who she was, what she was, when she finally exploded from within, screaming a string of unholy exclamations against the thin walls of the hotel room. Amy grabbed Ruby's left wrist with both hands and begged, "Please turn off the phone! Oh god, please turn it off!"

Ruby disconnected the call with Amy's cell and delicately fished inside Amy's other cell for her phone, carefully removing the slimy device. As soon as Ruby's hand was free of her cunt, Amy curled up on the damp sheets and sobbed.

"There, there," Ruby cooed, "Mommy's here."

After a few minutes, without turning around, Amy whispered, "I hope Youseff didn't hear me scream. I'm so ashamed."

"Uniceff? He's in the adjoining room?"

"Yeah, he's on the other side of the connecting door. It's a wonder he didn't burst in here when I screamed."

"It's okay, honey," Ruby said, rubbing Amy's arm. "You should try to get some sleep. Would you like Mommy to sing you a lullaby?"

Ruby got no response, thus she began her sweet song:

Fille Amy,
Fille Amy,
Dormez vous?
Dormez vous?
Sonnez les téléphones,
Sonnez les téléphones,
Buzz, buzz, buzz!
Buzz, buzz, buzz!

After a few solemn refrains, Amy was fast asleep with her thumb in her mouth...

***

When Amy suddenly awoke, she found herself in an empty room and immediately noticed that the connecting door was wide open. Still nude, but with her energy level *renewed*, Amy left the bed and crept toward the open door. A light was on in Youseff's room.

She was shocked by the sight of Youseff, tied naked to the bed with towels, and Ruby sitting naked on top of him, grinding away at his crotch. Slightly embarrassed, Amy thought about sneaking back to her room before they noticed her presence, but then she caught the glimmer of something behind Ruby's back.

Amy focused in to realize that one of Ruby's hands was behind her back and was holding a straight razor. The razor was only visible for a moment, because Ruby brought her arm back in front of her to show Youseff the blade.

"As soon as I come, you're gonna go, Uniceff," Ruby threatened. "I'm gonna slit your fuckin' throat, you pervert."

Knowing that it didn't take much to make the bitch come, Amy raced toward the bed, grabbing the Blenko Apple from the dresser on the way. Ruby had her back to Amy and didn't notice the younger woman's approach until she was at the bed.

Ruby turned her head to see what was behind her, only to witness the glass fruit smashing into her face, caving in her eye socket and sending shards of broken glass and bone into her brain. Ruby tumbled off Youseff and hit the floor hard with a thump.

But the thumping continued.

"What the fuck is that?" Youseff asked in a panic.

From outside the door, they heard a loud voice: "Open up, Youseff John! We know you're in there. We have a warrant for your arrest!"

The thumping on the door continued.

"Where's her razor? I need to cut you loose," Amy sputtered, looking on the bed and the floor for the blade.

The thumping on the door continued.

"There's no time for that," demanded Youseff. "Go back to your room and lock the door. They'll catch up with me eventually anyway."

"But what about my story?"

"Go, Amy, get the fuck out of here."

As Amy was escaping through the connecting door, the hotel manager was unlocking Youseff's room for the authorities. A group of state policemen burst into the room. They saw Youseff tied to the bed, although he had just freed his right hand by forcefully twisting the towel loose. They also saw Ruby dead on the floor, her blood oozing from her crushed skull.

"You sick fuck!" one of them said.

Youseff lifted his head slightly to respond. "I thought I had the Do Not Disturb sign out."

The elevator was overcrowded with the police officers and with Youseff, who was wearing a bathrobe, a pair of handcuffs and leg shackles. He didn't expect there to be anyone in the lobby during the early morning hours, since it was still dark outside, but he was wrong.

As soon as the elevator door opened into the lobby, a throng of reporters rushed toward him with video cameras, still cameras and still more cameras. Youseff was temporarily blinded by the flashing cameras as the officers in front of him forged a path through the lobby.

Reporter #1: Mr. John, how long did you think you could be on the run?

Youseff: No comment.

Reporter #2: Mr. John, did you kill all those women at the prison?

Youseff: *No comment.*

Reporter #3: Mr. John, could you tell us if those were your snuff films at the Serpents Club?

Youseff: *No comment*!

Reporter #4: Youseff, tell us what happened to your brother.

Youseff: I don't know! Leave me alone!

The press followed the perp and the police outside the hotel. The reporters continued to hurl a barrage of insensitive and hurtful questions at Youseff. He was quickly led to the side of a police cruiser.

As they were opening the back door to help Youseff inside the vehicle, Youseff caught a glimpse of Amy scurrying across Third Avenue. "Get in the car, sicko!" commanded an officer.

The last memory Youseff would have of his friend Amy was seeing her run down in the street by a yellow Ford F-150 Fx4, with a stainless steel brush guard, which sped off without stopping. The police had better things to do that morning.

A small minority of humans
Looked upon as eccentric,
Odd, even wicked, decided
To turn either right or left
Following little used paths,
And often overgrown paths.
These Paths of forbidden
Knowledge, wisdom and
Power.

- Written on the wall: Floor 2 Block B Cell 8

Meself never turned down an opportunity to tongue wrassle or swap spit with any bitch who was willing, but he was disgusted the next morning when he woke to the reality of a slobbering greyhound licking at his face.

"Oh yuck!" Meself spat. "Paul, call off your fucking dog!"

The frightened dog squeezed back between the front seats to rejoin the other dog and Paul in the rear of the van. Meself didn't wait for a response from Paul, but exited the van to find his favorite bush to relieve himself. Paul better not let those dogs piss in my van, Meself thought, as he looked out onto the Ohio River.

Now that Meself was fully awake and definitely living in the present, he decided to try to forget the strange happenings within the prison. After all, isn't it the American way to ignore things which you cannot comprehend?

Of course, there were still outstanding issues as far as Youseff's absence and Paul's presence that morning. Meself regretted arguing with his brother and allowing him to return to the prison by himself. He had hoped that Youseff would have shown up to report that all was well with the cast at the penitentiary and that the footage they had shot was secure.

Greyhounds were sniffing at his feet as he was pulling up his zipper. Paul wasn't too far behind; having managed to set up his cart on his own, so Meself restrained himself from kicking at the annoying hounds.

"Top of the morning to you, Citizen John."

"Whatever."

"Ahh, look, you can see the casino and racetrack from here. What did you say they were calling it now?"

"Wheeling Peninsula Casino and Racetrack."

"Yes, that was it. You know, by all rights, I should be runnin' that place. Big Bill Lias, the bastard who tried to blow me up in my car, bought Wheeling Peninsula when it was a horse track in nineteen-forty-five for a quarter million dollars. To his credit, he invested another half million into the place and turned it into the finest half-mile horse track in the country. Three years later, he had to give up ownership when the Feds accused him of owing two and a half million in back taxes. But the mob still continued to run the place. Look at it now. Ain't she a beauté?"

"I guess."

"So what's the game plan? When are we going to meet this Black Hand guy who runs Wheeling?"

"Just remember that this Black Hand guy is the one who bankrolled my movie and I'm not sure whether I have anything to show for it."

"Fuggit about it, I'll smooth that over for you."

"Paul, get real. How are you going to smooth anything over? You don't even know who this guy is."

"No, but I bet he knows *who I am* and that's all that counts."

"Yeah, and he'll probably start singing the refrains from '*Abbey Road*' that Paul is dead. So how are you going to explain that?"

"Because," he answered slowly. "Something… will… come together…."

"Right now," Meself interjected. "My main focus is getting something to eat. But we can't do that, since we don't have any money or credit cards. So that means I've got to go mooch some cash from a friend at the cathedral, because my bank is closed today. After that I think we should come back here to wait on Youseff, since the Serpents Club doesn't open until evening anyway."

"How about some steak and eggs at Zeller's on Market Street?"

"How about you stop living in the past?"

Later that day, Meself angled the van off Main Street and drove deep into the back of the desolate parking lot of the Downtown Inn. This is too much like Déjà vu, he thought, reminding himself that he wanted to fuggit about the Serpents Club.

After parking, Meself and Paul crossed over the path leading to the driveway of the Serpents Club and approached the back door. As soon as Meself knocked, they were greeted by a friendly "No dogs allowed" and the door was shut in their faces.

Meself tried again. When the door cracked open, Paul volunteered, "These are service dogs. I'm handicapped."

Still speaking anonymously through the crack, "Well, if you're blind, why do you want to go to a strip club?"

"I'm not blind and we have business with the Black Hand."

The door opened farther to reveal a woman in a bath robe, who was probably one of the strippers.

"The Black Hand won't be in tonight."

Meself spoke up, "Is Kay here?"

"No, she called off."

"Where can we find the Black Hand? We've got some urgent business with him," Paul stressed.

"If I was you, I'd try him at his day job tomorrow at the casino," she answered. "He's head of the Human Resources office."

"Thank you, ma'am."

While Paul and the dogs were re-boarding the van, Meself walked across the motel parking lot and found a payphone. He tried calling Kay's cell phone number, but got no response.

***

The Black Hand was about seventeen miles west of Wheeling that evening, and was pulling his black Cadillac Escalade into the Two Zero Eight Fuel Plaza on Interstate 70 near Belmont, Ohio. He'd placed an ad on Craigslist seeking women interested in working on an adult film. His SUV had a large magnetic sign on the driver's side door stating "Stargazer Productions."

The lot lizards began crawling around his expensive vehicle as soon as he parked in the dimly-lit area in the back of the truck stop, where most of the tractor trailers were located. The lot was abuzz with the steady humming of idling truck motors and unidle truck whores. The Black Hand would lower his driver's side window at the approach of each harlot.

Whether they'd heard about the Internet ad or not, the Black Hand sized up each slut and asked if they'd ever made a snuff film before. If they answered affirmatively, he'd consider them worthless liars and immediately roll his window back up. Some women aren't even worth the time and effort to kill.

But who was this sweet young thing approaching?

"Hey, Mister, are you the guy who placed the ad for the adult movie?"

"That's a big ten four," he answered in the lingo of the lot lizard.

"You mean two-oh-eight, right? I had a hell of a time finding this place. You should-a put the exit number in your ad."

"The exit number is two hundred and eight."

"Well, yeah, I know that now after I asked for directions like two hundred and eight times."

"Listen, honey, why don't you climb into the passenger side and we can talk more about the movie?"

The Black Hand checked out her body closely as she circled in front of his vehicle. The tiny white chick was about five and a half feet tall and was slender, sported small breasts and long blonde hair, and she appeared to be in her late teens. She wore a Cleveland Browns sweatshirt and brown jeans.

She jumped up into the front passenger seat once the Black Hand unlocked the door. He was glad that she didn't wait for him to get out of the car to open the door for her, because she'd still be waiting.

"Hi, my name is Paula Beverly, but my friends call me Peanut Butter."

"Hello, Miss Bailey, people just call me Dragon," he responded. "I'm glad you saw my ad."

Peanut Butter looked around the dark interior of the vehicle and observed, "This ain't one of them bait cars is it?"

"No, but from the looks of you, you might be jail bait."

"Nah, I ain't no jail bait. I turned eighteen like, well, like, ten minutes ago or something."

"That's what I thought."

"Hey, if you got a release form, I'll sign it. I don't give a shit. I just wanna make movies. I got me a great title for one too. How about *Peanut Butter and KY Jelly*?"

"I'm glad to see you're so enthusiastic. Do you know what a snuff film is?"

"You mean like a TV commercial for chewing tobacco?"

"Not exactly, but that's close. I'd like for you to do a screen test back at the studio in Wheeling tonight, unless someone's waiting on you to return this evening."

"Hell no, you could be some serial killer and leave me dead along the highway and nobody would miss me. Shit, no!"

The Black Hand smiled, "Are you sure you don't work for law enforcement?"

"I was gonna ask you the same fuckin' thing."

During the brief drive back to Wheeling, the Black Hand got to listen to a number of movie ideas from Peanut Butter, including one involving a black guy named Reeses. Unfortunately for the Black Hand, none of her plots included her getting cut into ribbons like peanut butter toffee.

"...Or like we could have some dude dressed as Elvis come up to me with his dick hanging out of like his rhinestone pants. His dick'll be covered in like peanut butter and he'll ask me if I wanna taste his peanut butter and banana sammich. And while I'm sucking him off, he could be singing that song from the Mall Boys, you know, 'It's Peanut Butter Jelly Time! Peanut Butter Jelly Time! Peanut Butter Jelly Time! Now break it down and freeze. Take it down to your knees.' Hey, speakin' of movies, did you ever see that old '*Tango and Cash in Paris*' flick where the guy demands butter because he wants to fuck the girl in the ass? We could do something like that, except the guy would ask for peanut butter... *and* I don't do anal. Really, I don't. Are you listening? I don't do anal. Anyway, here's another idea, you know how like they say peanut butter sticks to the roof of your mouth? Well, we could have some guy or some girl eatin' my pussy, and then pretending like they got stuck there. I'd say like, 'I guess it's true that peanut butter does stick to the roof of your mouth!' Or how about this? This is really kinky. I could be like a dominatrix, you know, dressed in leather and all that, and I could have this slave actin' like she or he was my fuckin' pet. You know, crawling around on all fours with a collar, begging for treats and stuff. Well, I'd spread peanut butter on my snatch and they'd have to lick it off, just like a real dog would. Then there's this scene, if we could find someone who looks like Jimmy Carter, you know that peanut farmer who became president and lusted after women in his heart and hated the Je…"

"We're here!" announced the Black Hand as he pulled into the driveway of the Serpents Club, which connected to the back parking lot shared by the Mary Isabella Apartments.

The Black Hand led the squawk box through the back door of the apartment building and into an empty studio style apartment – empty except for a massage table, a brand new Canon 1172 video camera and plastic covering the carpet.

"Why don't you strip off and lie belly down on the bench while I get the camera ready for the screen test?" he suggested as he closed the door to the apartment.

"Oh, I get it, a quick massage to loosen me up before the big test. I can get with that. Just remember, I don't do anal."

Peanut Butter quickly undressed, pulling off her sweatshirt to reveal no bra, her jeans to reveal no panties and her sneakers to reveal no socks. Consequently, her petite and pointy breasts and her sparsely-developed yellow pubic mound were immediately on display.

As the waif climbed up on the paper-covered table, the Black Hand realized that no one could ever call her chunky peanut butter. "I'll be ready in a jiff," he added.

"Hurry, 'cause it's kinda chilly up here."

As soon as the Black Hand had the camera properly positioned on the tripod and the record light on the front flashing green, he walked over to Peanut Butter. He knelt down beside the table and opened a small cabinet on the side.

"I'm going to see how you'll look on screen with handcuffs on," he announced.

"Ohhh, kinky," she responded as she felt him reach up and grab her leg, pulling it off the side of the table and snapping a cold metal cuff onto her ankle. He snapped the other side of the cuff onto a locked drawer handle.

He repeated the procedure with her other leg, and then secured her arms off the side of the table with another two pairs of handcuffs. Her arms and legs were draped over the sides of the massage table and her apple-shaped goosebump-covered ass was on full display.

"I guess you didn't like any of my movie ideas," she observed.

"I guess not," he agreed.

He stood in front of her, being careful not to block the camera shot, and grabbed a lock of her hair with his right hand.

"I want to get a good shot of your mouth for the oral scene," he told her. "You know, to make sure there's not a lot of rotten teeth or anything. Open your mouth toward the camera… open it wide… wiggle your tongue around… moisten your lips… lick the outside of your mouth, like you're lapping up some cum… that's it, keeping doing that… you're doing good."

In the moment that she blinked her eyes, she immediately felt a sharp pain on tip of her tongue. She opened her eyes wide to see the handles of a pair of pliers in the man's left hand. She started struggling, but couldn't move her head, even when he let go of her hair.

The Black Hand pulled on the girl's tongue until it extended as far as it could from her mouth, and then flipped open his straight razor with his right hand and severed off her tongue with one slice, deep inside her mouth.

"Ugh!" she screamed as blood began spurting from her mutilated mouth, while her arms and legs pulled and tugged vainly against the table.

The Black Hand tossed the bloody razor and the pliers on the floor. He grabbed the tongue with his right hand and did a little dance in front of the girl's panicked face, her eyes popping out in terror as she continued to choke on her own blood.

"Found a peanut, found a peanut, found a peanut just now, just now I found a peanut, found a peanut just now," he sang as he danced. "It was rotten, it was rotten, it was rotten just now…"

He laughed as he watched her horrified expression, enjoying the grunting and gurgling sounds coming from her mouth. He eventually stopped dancing and held the tongue up to his ear, like he was answering a phone.

"What did you say?" he asked, wagging the tongue against his ear like it was whispering to him. "I can't understand you. Stop flapping your tongue and talk to me! What? You like to speak in tongues? Well, that's your business. What? What now? Oh, you don't do anal? I know, you told me already. But I bet you wouldn't turn down a rim job, would you? What? What?"

He walked behind the table and reached under her hips with this right hand. He rubbed her tongue against her pussy, pressing it hard against the folds. The girl kicked hard with her legs, but only succeeded in cutting up her ankles inside the sharp cuffs.

"Yeah, that's it, a pussy licking for Peanut Butter. You like to have a tongue on your hot little pussy, don't you? Can you feel it on your clit? But don't you come, you hear? We're not near done yet. There's a little matter of a rim job that I promised you."

The Black Hand removed the tongue from her crotch and began circling the girl's anus with the tip. He waited for the orifice to loosen up a bit, but then realized that the girl's defensive instincts were keeping the sphincter tightly closed.

"You gotta loosen up, Peanut Butter," he encouraged. "You need to be more uninhibited if you want to be in my films."

Being the ever impatient lover, the Black Hand had to resort to pressing the tip of the tongue hard against her butthole, pressing down with his fingers, until the slick organ finally popped inside. The girl's body quit resisting at the point of penetration and went limp against the table. He scrambled to get the camera off the tripod for a close-up.

***

After a trip to the bank to withdraw some meager funds, Meself drove Paul to the Wheeling Peninsula Casino and Racetrack later in the morning. Paul doubted the casino would allow him to take his dogs through the gaming area, so he asked Meself to pull around the back of the facility where the dog track was located.

Lot G had a few buses parked around the perimeter, but there were very few cars using the lot because the races did not begin until noon. The walking path leading up to the racetrack was open for the early birds who wanted to get a jump on handicapping that afternoon's racing program.

Meself was adamant about not accompanying Paul into the facility, because he was worried about the Black Hand's reaction to his failed video shoot. Meself did help Paul onto his cart and attached the dogs.

"Make sure the reins are tight," Paul suggested. "I don't want any mishaps if there are other dogs around."

"Well, this is a dog racing track."

"Don't remind me."

Meself was soon watching Paul and his dogs roll up the paved walkway toward the indoor grandstand. Wanting to escape the crisp November morning air, Meself got back into the van to chill.

After waiting for a reluctant spectator to open the doors for him, Paul directed his dogs into the lobby, and past the betting machines, the snack bar and TV monitors. He found the door labeled Human Resources opposite the program sales booth.

Melvin "the Black Hand" Pike was inside the HR office with Robert "Little Codfish" Bricker and both were dressed in the latest José Bank two-for-one business suits. Pike was behind his tidy desk and was telling Bricker that he was anxious over last night's festivities, since he had played with his play date too long and did not have time to bury her in the backyard of the apartment building before dawn. Bricker was in the process of offering his assistance when they heard scratching at the glass door of the office.

Pike looked over to see two greyhounds pawing the glass. "What in the hell is that? Who brought those filthy hounds inside? Bob, check out who the fuck that is."

"Yes, sir."

As soon as Bricker opened the door, Paul wheeled into the office with his snarling, slobbering animals. "Greetings, gentlemen!"

"Who the fuck are you and why are you bringing those dogs into my office?"

"Now, hold your horses – no pun intended," Paul responded intentionally. "As you can see by my amended stature, I have a little trouble getting around on my own these days. But I do appreciate all the ramps and such that are strategically placed around the racetrack."

"So you came in here to thank us for the facility being handicap accessible? Well, you can thank the government for that, since it's the law."

"The law? The law? Did you say something about the law? Where are they?" Paul joked, twisting his head from side to side and breaking out into a loud laugh, while the full-sized men just stared at him in disbelief. "But seriously, the reason I'm here is to get a job, either in here or in one of your, well, let's just say, *less legitimate* outside endeavors."

"Bob, would you show this gentleman out of my office?"

As Bricker approached, Paul blurted, "Wait, wait, I've got a proposition to make that you'll definitely want to hear."

"All right," Pike conceded. "But make it quick – and your dogs better not shit on my floor."

Bricker sat back down in the chair facing the desk while the dogs began sniffing his shoes. Paul took the time to glance at the name plate on the desk.

"Melvin Pike," Paul read. "I told my boys you might be the Black Hand. I guess the gang up in Uniontown set you up real good while I was inside."

"I don't know what you're talking about," Pike said. "And if you've been incarcerated, you can forget about being hired on here, even if you are handicapped. As the suitability adjudicator of this facility, I've already determined that you lack the integrity, trustworthiness, reliability and good conduct standards required for employment at this establishment."

"Takes one to know one I guess," Paul shot back. "Don't tell me you don't know who I am. I'm Paul Hankish. I used to run this town."

Pike laughed, "You say you're Paul 'No Legs' Hankish? Seriously, that's what you want me to believe?"

"I am and I can prove it."

"Buddy, just because you're missing a couple limbs don't mean you can run around and play mobster. Besides, I heard Hankish died... and if he were alive he'd look a hell of a lot older than you."

"Well, you heard wrong. I'm alive, having aged gracefully, and I am in possession of the Grave Creek Stone."

The dogs whimpered at the words of their master, and then the room fell silent as Pike stared down at Paul, sizing up the half-sized man. The ringing of the phone on Pike's desk broke the silence. Pike picked up the receiver for a moment, and then placed it back on the cradle, disconnecting the call. For good measure, he pressed a couple of buttons to set up the line for voice messages.

"Do you have it?" Pike quietly asked.

"Have what?"

"The *stone*, you asshole. What do you think I meant?"

"I told you, it's in my possession."

"It's on you, right now? You have it on you?"

"Well, no, I don't have it in my pocket right now, if that's what you mean. But it's in my possession, like I said, and it's safe."

"So, what's your proposition?"

"Well, I'm willing to share the power of the stone if you're willing to share power over the city. With the stone at our disposal and the five families behind us, there will be no limitations on what we can accomplish in this godforsaken town… I'm only asking for what is rightfully mine."

"Rightfully yours? I'm still not convinced you are who you say you are. Maybe you're with the feds, trying to set me up?"

"Well, I do know that you couldn't use the stone even if you held it in your hands. You'd need the knowledge that's stored right up here in my head," Paul added, pointing to his skull, "and in my head alone."

"Is that right?" Pike answered, reaching for a cloth briefcase at his feet and placing it on the desk. "Well, if you're Paul Hankish, you should be familiar with this."

Pike opened the briefcase and removed a number of notebooks. He flipped through the pages of one notebook and presented an open page to Paul. The page contained a lot of unusual words, spelled out phonetically.

"Is this your handwriting?"

"Where did you get that? Those are my notebooks!"

"Not anymore they're not. This material was removed from your cell after you disappeared from the state pen in the seventies. The stuff has since come into my possession."

"But you still don't have the stone and I'm not dumb enough to carry it on me, like you do those notebooks."

"You're right, I don't have the stone and that's why I'm still listening to you, instead of tossing you off this property," Pike stated. "You said something earlier about 'your boys,' so are you expecting to get jobs for your crew too?"

"Nah, the John brothers don't work for me. We was just in the pen together for awhile. They're filmmakers or something stupid like that."

"The John brothers? Meseff and Youself, or whatever their fucked up names are?"

"Yeah, they said they had some kind of business deal with you as the so-called Black Hand."

"Well, right now those cocksuckers are on my shit list and they better not come anywhere near me. My sources tell me that some nastiness happened at the prison while they were filming their little skin flick. It hasn't been on the news yet, but once it breaks there's going to be a lot of heat on the adult entertainment venues in this town."

"No problem," Paul assured, "I'll make sure they stay away. One of them – the retarded one – is missing anyway."

Pike contemplated for a moment before moving his hands to the computer keyboard on his desk. He began clicking his mouse, scanning through some pages on the casino's personnel database. Paul watched the man play with the magical TV screen for a few minutes.

While Pike was working, Paul eventually looked over to Bricker. "I don't think we've been introduced," he said, reaching a hand up toward the man. "Like I said, I'm Paul Hankish."

Bricker looked down at the man, but ignored Paul's extended hand. "My name is Robert Bricker, if it's any of your concern."

"Bobby Bricker Junior!" Paul expounded, withdrawing his hand. "Your father, the Codfish, used to work for me. He was a good man. Boy, could I tell you some stories!"

"Who gives a shit?"

Pike cleared his voice to get the men's attention. "Actually, I think I found something for you, Hankish, if that's really your name. Do you happen to speak Korean?"

"No, I don't speak Korean."

"Well, that doesn't matter. How about I put you in charge of the retired greyhound adoptions?"

"What's that?"

"When the dogs go past their prime, we try to adopt them out to loving families in the community."

"Why don't you just kill 'em?"

"Well, we used to do that, but now the practice is frowned upon."

"Dog adoptions…I don't know…"

"Listen, Hankish, take it or leave it, beggars can't be choosers. I thought you'd appreciate the position, seeing how you use those hounds to pull you around."

"All right," Paul agreed. "Do I get my own office?"

"Yes you do," Pike answered. "The office is part of the kennel building beside the track. Bobby and I will show it to you."

The two and a half men left the Human Resources office just as the first race of the day was being announced over the public address system:

"Here comes Spunky! And they're off. Grade A greyhounds are out of the box. And at the break it's four, three, five, eight and one. Number four, Honey-Do, has the lead now. Six and eight go wide around the turn. Four is still out in front on the back stretch. Second is Every Bite and third is Front Page. One and seven are moving up on the inside to challenge. Going around the final turn, there's a fight to the finish… and at the wire, number four, Honey-Do, holds on! Four, five, three and one. The winner, number four, Honey-Do, is a chocolate Irish female. She runs out of the Nikko Lee Kennels and is trained by Kai Miro. Second place is number five,

Every Bite. Third place is number three, Front Page. And fourth is number one, Nothing Really Satisfies."

With all the spectators paying attention to the race by watching video monitors or gazing out the large windows of the facility, it was difficult for Paul to maneuver his dogs around the legs of all the oblivious grandstanders.

He almost lost control of the dogs when he tried to get them past the snack bar. Sniffing at the hotdogs and hamburgers grilling behind the counter, the dogs went into frenzy, which caused one small child to be knocked down and his hot pretzel snatched from his hand by the hungry hounds. The kid's parent retaliated by dumping a large decaf coffee with artificial creamer onto the dogs, causing the animals to yelp in pain and dash away pulling Paul behind them on the cart, which rolled over the unfortunate child's fingers.

The customers were cussing as the dogs barreled through the lobby, bouncing off their legs and knocking over their chairs and tables. Winning bet tickets flittered to the ground to mix amongst the losing tickets, which had already been discarded by losing bidders, forcing the winners to grovel on the floor seeking their spoils amidst a sea of squandered stakes.

Paul was thankful that Pike and Bricker were holding the doors open for him as he rolled outside with his dogs.

"What the hell was all the commotion in there?" Pike asked as he closed the door on the rising racket inside.

"I don't know," Paul answered. "I guess the favorite didn't place or something."

242

Paul was relieved to see that the competing greyhounds from the first race had already been led off the track and that there were no other distractions for his dogs. No spectators were standing out front by the track because of the cool weather.

Leaving the grandstand area, there was a cement pathway to the right, which ran along the outside of the first turn of the track and led directly to the large blue-roofed kennel building. On the side of the building was a glass door with a sign above reading "Greyhound Adoptions."

Pike unlocked the door, and the men and animals went inside. The office was fairly large and very neat in its appearance, which pleased Paul as he imagined himself behind the desk trying to figure out how to operate the computer. Photographs of happy children hugging befuddled dogs adorned most of the wall space.

Pike explained that the previous adoption director was a relative of the governor and had left the track to accept a government position in Charleston.

"You'll have plenty of time to get used to the office," Pike concluded. "Let me show you around the rest of the building."

As they were leaving the office, they heard the public address system introducing the dogs for the next race as the caretakers lined the dogs up on the track in front of the grandstand:

"Here are the entrees and post weights for the second race. Please note that the number eight dog, McColloch's Leap, has been scratched...Number one, Into the Night, a black female, fifty-eight pounds; number two, Hades on Ice, a white-ticked red male, sixty

pounds; number three, Pomegranate Moth, a dark brindle female, sixty-seven pounds; number four, Forever Ago Sunshine, a red fawn dog, seventy-one pounds; number five, Karnivali, a white-ticked brindle female, seventy-nine pounds; number six, Cotton Mouth, a cream male, seventy-five pounds; and number seven, Lester's Ominous Gift, a blue fawn, sixty-nine pounds."

Paul followed the other two men as they walked toward the back side of the building, which was close to the point where the first turn of the track ended and a straightaway began. They were now out of sight of the spectators while the kennel staff was busy with the dogs on the track.

"So what's back here?" asked Paul.

"This is where you're going to tell me the location of the Grave Creek Stone," Pike answered as Bricker pulled a long silencer-equipped pistol from his sports coat and held it at Paul's head. "You can either tell me where the stone is, and enjoy your new job at the track, or Bobby's going to put a bullet in your head and throw what's left of your body in that manure bin over there."

Paul started stammering as the PA system announced the start of the race:

"Here comes Spunky! And they're off. Grade C greyhounds are out of the box. One has the lead, and then it's seven, six, four, three and five. As we come up to the turn, Into the Night has the advantage, then Lester's Ominous Gift. Karnivali is coming up on the inside to make a bid..."

Paul's dogs were ignoring their master's plight as they looked through the open gate leading out onto the track. The mechanical white rabbit buzzing around the first turn immediately caught their attention and Paul immediately tightened his grip on the reins as he was almost pulled off the cart. Before Bricker could squeeze the trigger, Paul vanished from underneath his sites in a burst of dust and gravel.

"...Wait! It looks like two more dogs have joined the race! Is one these dogs the one that was scratched? And what are they pulling behind? Some kind of ugly doll on a sulky? Is this some kind of prank? The new dogs are coming up fast on the pack from the outside as they near the last turn. The cart looks like it's about to flip in the turn, so they're taking it wide while the official dogs keep their pace on the inside. Oh, shit, now it looks like the dogs with the cart are headed out the back gate by the boxes! What the fuck is going on here? Meanwhile, number one is maintaining its lead into the final stretch..."

In the parking lot, Meself was bored and half asleep in the van, but had started perking up once his favorite Jefferson Airplane song came on the radio. He was casually singing along with the song, crooning, "And if you go chasing rabbits and you know you're going to fall..."

Then out of the corner of his eye, he caught sight of Paul and his dogs tearing down the pathway leading to the parking lot. Paul's face was as white as a five-star hotel sheet and it appeared as if Paul had no control over the running dogs.

Meself put the van into reverse gear in order to back out of his space and pursue the runaway dog cart, but he almost backed into a yellow Ford pick-up which was speeding through the lot behind him. Meself allowed the truck to get past him before he tried pulling out again. As he was shifting the van into drive, Meself realized that the yellow truck was already pursuing the dog cart.

Inside the truck, Pike was barking commands to Bricker behind the wheel. "There they are up there turning right onto Penn Street. Hurry up; we can't let him get away!"

"All right, all right, remember this truck ain't technically mine. I don't want to hit any cars in the parking lot."

"Fuck that! Just catch up to those dogs!"

Paul allowed the dogs to drag him down South Penn Street past Capo Di Tutti Capi's Gentleman's Club and Deli, but he saw backed up traffic beyond the intersection so he worked the reins hard to force the bridled dogs to cut left onto Ohio Street, flying haphazardly past the Voo Doo Lounge.

A tractor trailer was crossing the street in front of Spunky's Market, but the dogs never slowed down, running underneath the truck and causing Paul to duck down to clear the bottom of the trailer. Bricker had to pound down on the brakes to avoid smashing into the tractor trailer; and then had to wait until it cleared the roadway, which gave Meself time to catch up in the van.

Realizing they were being pursued, Paul quickly had his dogs turn right onto South Huron Street, and then hang another right onto busy Zane Street in front of Abby's Restaurant. Frustrated motorists blasted their horns when the dog cart ignored the traffic light and jumped onto Zane Street toward the bridge crossing the Ohio River.

When Bricker and Pike approached the intersection, Bricker asked which way they should go… "Go, go, go, right toward the city, stupid!" Pike screamed.

Children trying to cross the street had to leap out of the way of the yellow truck as it forced its way through the intersection. Before the frightened kids could catch their breath, Meself knocked a couple of them out of the way as he tore through behind the truck.

Paul and his dogs were now on the interstate and keeping pace with the speeding traffic all around them. Drivers dropped their cell phones when they saw the two dogs pulling the man across the bridge, flabbergasted over how a person could show such utter disregard for safety while on the road.

Paul kept the dogs in the right lane so that he could take Exit 1A into downtown. The ramp put him onto Main Street and the dogs rambled past the Mary Isabella Apartments and the Serpents Club. Paul realized he'd made a mistake in his getaway plan when he looked back to see the yellow truck approaching about two blocks behind.

Paul decided to get out of Pike's home turf, so he pulled left on the reins near the Downtown Inn, which put him on 10th Street for a block, and then another quick left put him on Market Street heading uphill. Having more control over the dogs allowed him to weave in and out of the heavy downtown traffic, while the yellow truck and white van had to wait behind.

"Son of a bitch, he's getting away!" Pike yelled. "Can't we fucking jump the curb or something?!"

"There's nowhere to go, even on the fucking sidewalk! We're stuck! We have to wait it out!" Bricker responded, throwing his hands up in frustration.

Pike reached over to the abandoned wheel and began blowing the horn, screaming out the open window for everyone to get out of their motherfuckingcocksucking way. Meself's van was about two cars back from the yellow truck and he was grateful that he was not in their motherfuckingcocksucking way.

Paul was worried that his dogs were tiring as they climbed the steep hill of upper Market Street. Soon the traffic light turned in his pursuers' favor and the chase was on again. Paul began slashing the reins against the dogs' backs, yelling out, "Mush, you bitches, mush!"

The yellow truck was gaining on Paul and the dogs as they reached the Stone Boulevard intersection at the top of the hill. The traffic light was just turning red, but Paul crossed through anyway, causing a rear-end collision for two drivers who believed they had the right-of-way. Bricker stopped at the red light even though Pike did not agree with his decision.

Bricker and Pike were forced to sit and watch as Paul's cart hit a pot hole near the Begging Mingo statue. Paul lost his grip on the reins and had to grab the front of his cart to keep his balance and not be thrown into traffic. The dogs kept running, spooked by the crashing cars and the honking horns. Desperate to get off the roadway, the dogs ran toward a gap in the fence near a historic marker on the right side of the street. They blindly dashed through the broken fence, running on nothing but air as they leapt off the edge of the embankment, carrying Paul behind them.

Waiting at the intersection in his mom's car, one toddler, who was too young to be sitting in the front seat of his mother's car, pointed at the scene unfolding in front of him and proclaimed, "Look mommy, it's the Grinch who stoled Christmas!"

When the light changed, Bricker cautiously turned left and slowly drove past the gap where Paul had flown off the precipice of the hillside. Meself, who also saw the suicide jump, decided to turn right and park in the abandoned lot of the Old Windmill Pub. Since there was still a lot of turmoil at the scene of the collision, Meself was able to sneak out of the van and walk unobserved across the street to get a better look at where Paul disappeared into oblivion.

Pike had Bricker turn into the parking lot of the Leap Café at the bottom of the hill and they both got out of the truck to scrutinize the strange turn of events. They walked to an old railroad bridge crossing over Wheeling Creek and looked up at the steep hillside rising 300 feet to the top of Market Street.

"Ain't no way he survived that," Bricker commented.

"Yeah, but where's the body? I don't see where he crashed down."

"The way he flew off the cliff, I think he could've hit the crick. Him and his dogs surely have drowned."

"Probably, but I think we should still take a walk upstream to see if we can find anything."

"No problem, boss."

As they started their fruitless trek along the creek, Pike concluded, "After this, we're going to find those John brothers and kill them, but only after they tell us where Hankish hid the stone."

"What if they don't know about the stone?"

"They both die, regardless of the stone, and regardless of how long it takes to find the bastards. The deader they are, the less heat'll be on the organization."

***

Meself fled the scene once the cops arrived. He took some back streets to get to his back alley sanctuary by the Ohio River. Meself had never hoped so much to find Youseff waiting for him than he did that day; but when he arrived, Youseff was still nowhere to be found.

Meself parked the van and shut off the engine, and then leaned his seat back. He felt another headache coming on. Having not experienced any head trauma lately, he credited the burgeoning headache to either stress or a lack of food.

He closed his burning eyes and thought about Youseff. He thought about Youseff and the way Youseff used to eat like a fucking hog. He thought about Youseff and the way Youseff used to eat like a fucking hog –and store food in the back of the van in an old Styrofoam cooler. He thought about checking the cooler to see if there was any unrotten food which he could partake of in Youseff's absence.

Meself reluctantly climbed into the back of the van, cussing when he stepped in what appeared to be dog shit, and found the filth-covered cooler. He popped the lid off, but only saw one aluminum foil wrapped item inside.

It was heavy, which made Meself's stomach turn in disgust, but he unwrapped the mystery item anyway. Soon Meself held in his hand the coveted Grave Creek Stone. He felt the smoothness of the cold stone and studied its inscriptions.

"I bet I could skip this thing halfway across the Ohio," he said to himself.

But then Meself remembered what Paul had apparently been able to do with the stone when they were all inside the Indian mound. Perhaps if he turned the stone over to the Black Hand, the mobster would forgive his failed film project? He decided to find a fast food restaurant, which still had a payphone, so that he could get something to eat and attempt to give Kay another call.

Meself was able to connect with Kay, but she was not a happy camper and she cussed him for abandoning the video shoot. She kept asking him if he was aware of what happened at the prison and if he knew whether Youseff was safe, but Meself insisted that he didn't know anything.

Kay wanted to hang up and tell him never to call her again, but Meself begged her to tell the Black Hand about the Grave Creek Stone. Before he finished his McRib, he heard the payphone ringing and discovered that the Black Hand wanted him to drop off the stone at the Serpents Club that evening.

When Meself arrived at the club at the appointed time, he was surprised to see a Closed sign on the back door. He knocked anyway and was soon face to face with Kay, who was dressed casually in jeans and a buttoned blouse. The club was dark – darker than usual, but Meself found his way to the bar by following Kay.

From behind the bar, Kay announced, "The Black Hand will forgive the money you wasted on the film if you give me the stone."

Meself wasted no time in handing her the stone, which she studied in the dim light and laughed while she shook her head. She bounced it in her hand like it was a toy.

"Be careful with that," Meself warned. "It can conjure up spirits and raise the dead."

"Is that right?" she asked, rolling her eyes.

"Hell, yes, I've witnessed its power," he added. "So, if he wanted to, the Black Hand could kill you and then use the stone to reanimate you as a sort of zombie slave."

Kay put the stone under the counter and grabbed a remote.

"Have you been watching much TV today?"

"I don't have a TV, why?"

"Let's see if it's still on…"

A television mounted to the wall snapped on, brightening the room a bit. The local news was still covering the massacre at the prison. A reporter was saying that a number of bodies were found at the prison yesterday morning and the police were still looking for witnesses.

Meself was stunned. "Oh my god, what about Youseff?"

"Youseff? I believe Youseff made it out through that tunnel you discovered," Kay said. "But what are *you* going to say when the cops track you down?"

Panicked, Meself began sweating, and pleaded, "Well, you gotta help me or you gotta get the Black Hand to help me. Maybe he knows a place where I can hide out or something?"

"I don't *gotta* do anything," she stated, matter-of-factly. "And giving you sanctuary was not part of the deal for the stone."

"Please, Kay, can't you do me this favor?"

"Why should I help you after what you did to me?"

"I didn't do anything to you."

"You don't remember, do you?"

"What, Kay? What don't I remember? Whatever it is, I'll make it up to you, I swear."

"You don't remember these?"

Kay grabbed the front of her blouse with both hands and ripped it open, sending buttons bouncing against the bar and Meself. He stared at her exposed chest and instantly remembered the pentagram tattoos over the nipples.

"Now do you remember? Do you remember raping me in my own bedroom while your brother filmed it?"

"Oh, my god, Kennedy."

"I don't go by Kennedy anymore. Kennedy was a victim, but Kay isn't. After you raped me, I changed everything I could about myself to try to forget. I even shaved my fucking head so that I could look at myself in the mirror again!"

Before Meself could even try to apologize, Kay grabbed a large carving knife from behind the bar and buried it in Meself's chest. Shocked by the sudden action, Meself looked down at the quivering knife handle protruding from his chest and felt his shirt getting drenched with blood. Just before he fell from the bar stool, he muttered, "Point taken."

Kay casually picked up the stone and walked around the bar. Being careful not to slip on any blood, she stepped over Meself's body and headed toward the front door of the club. She picked up a windbreaker jacket from one of the tables to cover herself.

Once she was outside in the chilly November air, she grabbed her cell phone from her back pocket and called her boss. He drove by within minutes to retrieve the stone.

"Thank you, Kay. Can you handle the clean-up in the club, while I take this next door?" he asked as she handed the stone through the window of the Escalade.

"I suppose," she answered. "I got nothing better to do."

Before re-entering the Serpents Club, Kay walked around the back of the building and retrieved a wheelbarrow, which she managed to push inside the club. Following the Black Hand's recommendations, she unrolled some plastic on the floor beside Meself's body and rolled the bloody dead man onto the sheet. She then stripped her victim and mopped up the spilled blood from the part of the floor where Meself had leaked.

To make her chore less monotonous, she muted the television and turned on some heavy metal music. Listening to heavy metal always helped her pass the time while doing her school homework, so she figured it should also lessen the tediousness commonly associated with chopping up a dead body.

Wearing a disposable rain coat and armed with a meat cleaver, Kay set to work on Meself's body. If all went well during this practice exercise, her mom could very well be next on the chopping block.

"Now, now, now," she spoke to Meself. "If all this reanimation, back from the dead, talk is true, we've got to make sure you're in enough pieces that all the King's horses and all the King's men will never be able to put your sorry ass back together again... Hey, is this the left hand that grabbed my shorts so they could be cut off from me on the night I was raped? I believe you also slapped me across the face with that hand. Well, you won't be needing that anymore [chop]. And there's your right hand, which you held your knife with and used to shove that rosary and incense into my body. Sorry, that'll have to go too [chop, chop]. And don't look at me like that, with that smirk of yours. I remember your ugly face leaning down over me and biting my nipples. You didn't think I forgot about that, did you? What was it the Queen of Hearts used to say? Oh, yes, I remember now! Off with your fucking head, you bastard! [chop, chop, chop]..."

Speaking of the dead, the Black Hand was also visiting some perishable remains. "I sure hope my Peanut Butter hasn't gone too far over its expiration date," he observed as he entered the apartment with his briefcase.

Peanut Butter was still strapped face down to massage table, just like the Black Hand had left her the previous morning. Even though she was currently dead, the Black Hand checked her restraints before moving on to set up the video camera. He moved the tripod around the back end of the table, away from Peanut Butter's blood-caked and skewered face.

When he was satisfied with the set up and had the camera running, the Black Hand opened his briefcase and removed a notebook and the Grave Creek Stone. Dropping the briefcase to the floor, he struggled to hold the notebook open to the desired page with his left hand and clutch the stone in his right.

"Kit anamikon mani, mweckineckagoian kitcitwa oniciciiwewin; kije manito ki mamawiitim; kakina endactiwatcikwewak kin awacamenj ki kitcitwawinigo, gaie kitcitwawina jesos ka anicinabewiitisotc kiiawing."

The Black Hand glanced over the top of the notebook to observe Peanut Butter's body, but could not perceive any difference in her persistent passivity. He wasn't close enough to notice her rapid eye movement.

"Kitcitwa mani, kije manito wekwisisimate gaganotamawicinam neta pataiang, nongom gaie wi nipoiang gaganotamawicinam."

He did notice the groaning, almost immediately. The notebook was shaking in his hand as he looked over once again at Peanut Butter, whose body was beginning to convulse. The groaning then turned to gagging and the Black Hand watched as Peanut Butter coughed up a large blood clot from her mouth, spitting it onto the plastic-covered floor.

He struggled to find the final phrase on the wavering notebook in front of him, being more anxious than scared at the current stomach-turn of events. Believing it was possible to raise the dead, and actually witnessing it, proved to be two very different states of perception.

"Kekona ki ingi!"

Peanut Butter was once again fighting against her bonds on the massage table and the Black Hand was drooling with insatiable, omnipotent lust. He knelt down, never taking his eyes off his conquest's thrashing body, and carefully placed the notebook and stone on the top of his briefcase. As he stood back up, he already had his hand on his zipper.

Walking around behind Peanut Butter, he grabbed her hips and pulled them as close to the edge of the table as possible. "What was that you were saying about anal sex?" he asked.

As he jammed his lack-lubed lust into her dry ass cavity, she continued her haunting moans. He wondered if she could feel her body being viciously and violently violated, or was incessant moaning just something which came par for the course in raising the dead?

One distinct thing that he could feel, which scared him at first, almost causing him to pull out in terror, was a strong tickling sensation on the tip of his cock. Every time he drove his dick deep inside her ass, he could feel the incredible sensation on his knob. Rather than continue his piston-like fucking of her horrid hole, he was tempted to leave his cock buried in her ass for longer periods of time, because the sensation was driving him crazy with desire. He loved when a girl's spirited tongue licked the tip of his dick.

Outside, near the east bank of the Ohio River, Kay was finishing up tossing bits and pieces of Meself's body into the dark, murky waters. At first, the pieces just plopped into the river without disturbing the surface, but soon splashing could be heard after each part was tossed into the watery void. Kay knew the splashing was from the hungry catfish which ruled the Ohio's ecosystem, their reputations as bottom-feeders being relinquished in their desperate search for food. The four- and five-foot long blue catfish needed nourishment and Meself was happy to oblige of himself.

Kay's arms and legs were sore as she pushed the empty wheelbarrow back up toward the Serpents Club, opting to push the tool through the backyard of the Mary Isabella Apartments, since the yard was shrouded by bushes and it couldn't be seen in the moonlight from the upper floors of the nearby Downtown Inn.

Her legs felt weak and she had the sensation that the ground was giving way under her feet. The yard had a slight incline up toward the building, but Kay thought it wouldn't be a problem since the contents of wheelbarrow had been emptied into the river. Halfway up the yard, it seemed as if she couldn't proceed any farther. She considered abandoning the wheelbarrow, but thought she could instead rest a moment before continuing her trek.

She reached down to massage an aching ankle. Another hand grabbed her wrist, pulling her to the ground, using Kay as leverage to slowly pull itself out of the soil. Kay screamed in horror as she watched a body slowly emerge from the cold earth.

Kay felt the earth rumbling to her left and to her right, as two more bodies clawed themselves out from the depths of their shallow graves. All three dirt-covered bodies crawled toward the warmth which represented Kay's quivering being.

"My god, what have you done, Melvin?" she blurted out as the putrid bodies surrounded her, moaning in the frigid night air.

They climbed on top of Kay, covering her in their stench and rotting flesh, smothering her into certain oblivion. She felt their cold bodies sucking the warmth and life from her, icy fingers and hands covering her face and head.

"Stop!" Kay suddenly yelled out with authority, remembering her oath to never again be a victim.

The moaning mountain of immortality halted its attack at the sound of Kay's commanding voice.

"I'm not the one you want," Kay commanded. "The man who killed you and wants to control you is inside that building...up there. Follow the lights and you'll find him. Now leave me be!"

Kay found the strength to push the bodies off her and was relieved to see them begin their new journey toward the back of the Mary Isabella Apartments. As the creatures crawled away, Kay would lie upon on the dying grass, her back protected by her plastic poncho, close her eyes and murmur, "I bet you didn't even lock the door, did you Melvin?"

***

Her pupils adjusted to the harsh light inside the apartment well before her mind adjusted to the harsh realities flooding her brain receptors, specifically the sensory data capturing the unsavory scene unfolding before her blinking eyes... Nasty naked zombie zoetropes, scratching, slashing, stabbing hands into the screaming, slumping, struggling man in terror... Torn, twisted, tightening tendons snapping, separating, striating... Limbs pulled asunder like lambs to the slaughter, spraying, splashing, squirting blood and gore across the floor. The Black Hand shrieked as blacker hands pressed their filthy fingers deep inside his eye sockets, producing pain upon pulse-stopping, eye-popping, pain.

Kay side-stepped the mounting mayhem, ignoring even the tongueless tauntings of the still ensnared strumpet gyrating and grinding on the massage table, as she made her way to the Canon 1172 video camera. She panned and zoomed and positioned the camera to capture every sickening second of the Black Hand's impending demise.

"Hey," Kay yelled out to the players as the scene wound down. "Y'all passed the audition!"

EPILOGUE

The Intelligencer

Violent Protest on Lafayette

MOUNDSVILLE – A protest got out of hand Sunday evening at the W-Mart Super Center on North Lafayette Avenue in Moundsville, resulting in numerous injuries and at least one death. Police were contacted, but arrived on scene after the protestors had left the store.

Witnesses reported that a group of three to four protestors, dressed as Native American Indians, ran into the store shouting in a foreign language. The protestors reportedly began grabbing merchandise, such as knives and other tools, and attacking customers with the implements. Neither children nor the elderly were spared from the protestors' angry wrath, according to eye witnesses.

One witness reported seeing a customer's decapitated head being carried by a protestor atop a bamboo Tiki torch, which were on sale this weekend.

As many residents will recall, protests were a common occurrence at the site prior to the construction of the shopping center, specifically because the site was determined to contain an ancient Adena Indian burial mound. The corporation won a long court battle over the right to build on the site, however, and there had been no further protests since the store opened.

"Actually, the protestors looked like real Indians, but I bet they were from that hippy commune up on two-fifty," commented Wheeling resident Kennedy Schmulbach, who was on the scene with a video camera when the massacre occurred. She said she was scouting out locations for her MIA Film Company when the incident began.

ABOUT THE AUTHOR

After an unillustrious print journalism career in southwestern Pennsylvania, Rich Bottles Jr. moved to West Virginia at the age of 32 to pursue a career in technical writing. He spends his free time visiting and hiking at the many state parks in the Mountain State, which is also where he develops the concepts for his novels. He has produced a trilogy of WV-themed "humorrorotica" and is currently working on a romantic Appalachian horror story set in a quiet Amish community. His only regret in life is that his out-of-state secondary school education prohibited him from earning West Virginia's prestigious Golden Horseshoe Award.

Other great titles from:

www.BurningBulbPublishing.com

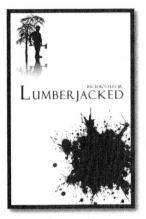

Lumberjacked
by Rich Bottles Jr.

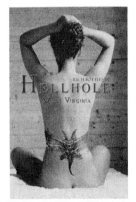

Hellhole West Virginia
by Rich Bottles Jr.

Available at www.BurningBulbPublishing.com
or scan the QR code to learn more on amazon.com.

Darkened Hills
by Gary Lee Vincent

Available at www.BurningBulbPublishing.com
or scan the QR code to learn more on amazon.com.

The Big Book of Bizarro
Edited by Rich Bottles Jr.
and Gary Lee Vincent

Vulgarity For The Masses
by J.S. Lawhead

Available at www.BurningBulbPublishing.com
or scan the QR code to learn more on amazon.com.

Printed in Great Britain
by Amazon